THE TRYST

Michael Dibdin was born in 1947, attended schools in Scotland and Ireland and universities in England and Canada. He spent four years in Italy where he taught at the University of Perugia, and he now lives with his wife and daughter in Oxford. His other titles are *The Last Sherlock Holmes Story*, *A Rich Full Death*, *Ratking*, *Dirty Tricks*, *The Dying of the Light* and *Dead Lagoon*.

In 1988, *Ratking* won the Crime Writers' Association Gold Dagger Award for the Best Crime Novel of the Year. Michael Dibdin reviews regularly for the *Independent on Sunday*.

by the same author

THE LAST SHERLOCK HOLMES STORY

A RICH FULL DEATH

RATKING

VENDETTA

CABAL

DIRTY TRICKS

THE DYING OF THE LIGHT

DEAD LAGOON

MICHAEL DIBDIN

The Tryst

faber and faber
LONDON · BOSTON

First published in 1989
by Faber and Faber Limited
3 Queen Square London WC1N 3AU
This paperback edition first published in 1990

Photoset by Parker Typesetting Service Leicester
Printed in England by Clays Ltd, St Ives plc
All rights reserved

© Michael Dibdin, 1989

This book is sold subject to the condition that it shall not, by way of trade or otherwise, be lent, resold, hired out or otherwise circulated without the publisher's prior consent in any form of binding or cover other than that in which it is published and without a similar condition including this condition being imposed on the subsequent purchaser.

A CIP record for this book
is available from the British Library

ISBN 0–571–14221–4

6 8 10 9 7

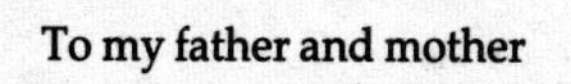

To my father and mother

Every crime has something of the dream about it. Crimes *determined* to take place engender all they need: victims, circumstances, pretexts, opportunities.

PAUL VALÉRY

ONE

'One of my patients thinks somebody's trying to kill him.'

She had meant to sound light and casual, but the words gushed out, breathless and urgent, betraying her feelings, her emotion, her involvement. It had been madness to mention the boy.

Or perhaps I'm imagining it, she thought. Perhaps he's noticed nothing.

Her husband speared one of the rectangles into which he had previously divided his slice of quiche, dredged it thickly in mayonnaise and hoisted it into his mouth. After chewing conscientiously for a moment or two, he glanced over at his wife.

'Isn't that fairly . . . normal?'

It was a trap, of course. If she took him literally, he would claim that he'd been joking; if she treated it as an example of the pawky humour he was so proud of, he would ask pointedly what was funny about someone in fear of his life.

'A normal delusion, you mean?' Aileen asked as she refilled their glasses with wine.

Her husband paused judiciously.

'Well, I take it that the person in question . . .'

'His name's Gary. Do finish the quiche if you can.'

She watched as Douglas lifted the remaining segment of quiche to his plate, then thrust his knife deep into the jar of mayonnaise.

'I take it that he *is* mad,' he concluded.

'"Mad" is no longer a recognized psychiatric category,' his wife replied primly.

'Well, psychosocially disadvantaged, or whatever the current jargon is. Observing non-normative behavioural criteria, into a whole other perceptual thing, marching to the beat of a different . . .'

'He's suffering from depression following an extremely stressful experience,' Aileen went on even more stiffly. She realized too late that she had been outmanoeuvred, boxed into a corner, a po-faced Aunt Sally glaring disapprovingly at her husband's puckish jests.

Douglas Macklin mopped up the remaining mayonnaise with his last soggy piece of quiche.

'What happened to him?'

'He witnessed a murder, actually.'

For a moment, her husband looked genuinely interested.

'Really?'

'Well, he found the body, anyway.'

She knew the risk she was taking, but it made no difference, not where the boy was concerned. The pressure of unspoken words was too great to be denied.

'His social worker referred him as query schizophrenic, but . . .'

'Now hang on a moment,' her husband interrupted with a frown. 'Schizophrenia. What *is* that, exactly?'

'Sorry?'

Douglas Macklin repeated his question.

'Oh, come on!' his wife urged with a laugh that sounded almost natural. 'Have you forgotten all those long discussions we used to have about it?'

Forgetting, as she well knew, was not something Douglas Macklin permitted himself to do.

'About *what*?' he hedged.

'About schizophrenia! That's what we're talking about, isn't it?'

'I wasn't absolutely sure what you were talking about, to be perfectly honest. That's why I asked the question.'

Aileen locked her teeth together. She had already said far too much. Yes, it had been madness to think that she could afford the luxury of discussing this, of all cases, with her husband, of all people.

'As to those discussions, I haven't forgotten them,' Douglas went on with renewed energy. 'Although it must be, what, almost twenty years ago now?'

He paused for a reminiscent smile.

'I seem to remember you arguing that madness is just a

strategy, a way of coming to terms with a crazy world. That the people we call mad are really *too* sane, so much so that the rest of us drive them mad. Tell me, do you still subscribe to that view? It's no longer quite so fashionable as it used to be, I believe.'

He spoiled things slightly by helping himself to more mayonnaise, which he ate with a piece of bread, ignoring the salad she had prepared. A parsimonious lower-middle-class upbringing in Aberdeen had left Douglas Macklin with a perpetually unsatisfied child inside, subject to indiscriminate greed that had no effect on his scrawny figure. Left to his own devices, Aileen knew, he would eat standing up at the kitchen counter, stuffing himself with lard sandwiches and sticky buns, washed down with mugs of hot sweet tea.

'Of course!' she snapped. 'You know me. I just parrot whatever idea is currently fashionable.'

She checked herself there, but it was too late.

'I didn't say that,' her husband recited slowly, as though dictating a letter to a not-very-bright secretary. 'I was merely asking about your views on a subject of professional interest. What's wrong with that?'

She said nothing.

'Honestly, Aileen, I'm beginning to worry about you, you know. You seem to get things completely out of proportion sometimes. To overreact grotesquely.'

He completed his triumph with a look both solicitous and critical.

There had been a time, earlier in their marriage, when Aileen had thought of the contests which took place at their dinner table every evening as a kind of psychological chess. She had soon come to realize that this image was totally inadequate. It was more like mud-wrestling than chess; intimate, bruising, slimy, devious and degrading. Facing her husband across the ruins of yet another meal, she asked herself once again how she came to be there, what it was that had brought her to that point. They had met in 1968 at the University of Sussex, where Douglas was finishing a BSc in what he liked to describe as 'the chemical soup we carry round in our skulls'. Aileen, too, was studying the brain, although from a different direction. She could have done her degree in psychology somewhere safe like Exeter, as her parents had wished, but the much-publicized high jinks of the glittery Sussex students tempted her to apply there. Eight months later, she was depressed, lonely, overworked, underfed and homesick. Out of season, Brighton proved to be cold and cheerless. The flat she was sharing with two other girls was smelly and damp, in particular the room which she had been allocated, and to make matters worse, her social life obstinately refused to take off. This was the more unbearable in that her flatmates were constantly being called for, taken out and brought back at all hours, or even not till the next morning. Aileen was cast in the role of housekeeper, taking messages and passing on directions, handing over keys and notes, making excuses, telling lies and answering the telephone, which never rang for her. Such invitations as she *did* receive were of a kind she could hardly flaunt before the Londoners, such as her tutor's Saturday morning 'at home'. Nevertheless it was there, amidst saucers of over-salted peanuts, thimbles of Cyprus sherry and sterile acres of strenuously intelligent conversation, that Aileen was introduced to Douglas Macklin.

Aileen had actually felt quite excited to be at the reception, until it dawned on her that attendance was virtually obligatory and everyone else was wondering how soon they could decently leave. The realization that she was the only person present who didn't have something more interesting to do brought on a crippling attack of self-pity, and so she felt quite grateful to the skinny sandy-haired Scotsman who talked her ear off about his work for the best part of an hour. When they said goodbye, he noted her address and phone number as impersonally as an estate agent. She was therefore quite surprised to be rung a few days later and asked out to the cinema. The following week Douglas invited her to a restaurant whose pretensions were reflected in the oppressive furnishings and overbearing service rather than the food. Afterwards they went to a pub to unwind, and when they reached the flat Aileen invited him in for coffee. When her trendy flatmates burst in with the usual admiring crew in tow, Aileen abruptly decided that she would not be sleeping alone that night. Although not technically a virgin, she had never been to bed with a man before, but it proved to be remarkably similar to what she had imagined. Douglas monopolized the action much as he had at her tutor's party, and as on that occasion Aileen was neither overwhelmed nor disappointed, merely grateful for the attention. When she got up to make tea in the morning, she knew that the other girls would never be able to impose on her in quite the same way again.

The affair staggered on for the rest of the academic year, although Aileen's commitment to it was progressively undermined by the confidence and assurance she had tasted for the first time that morning. She would have broken off their relationship eventually, if it hadn't become clear that it was dying a natural death. Douglas was going to London to do research at the Institute of Neurology, and although they made vague plans to see each other, nothing definite had been arranged by the time Aileen took off with a girlfriend to hitchhike to Greece. When she returned to Brighton in October, she met Raymond, a literature student from California who introduced her to marijuana, acid-rock music, anchovies, reincarnation, William Blake, tie-dyed T-shirts, peanut butter, Zen parables and oral sex.

When Aileen thought of Raymond now, it was the ghostly resemblance between him and her young patient, Gary Dunn, which compelled her attention: a resemblance all the more eerily disturbing for being fortuitous. But at the time, of course, she had known nothing of the horrors to come. Then, it had been Raymond's resemblance to his predecessor in Aileen's life which had struck her. Like Douglas, the American was over six feet tall, lithe but unathletic, with russet hair, grey-blue eyes and a weak chin. The similarity ended there, however. It was not simply that Raymond had shoulder-length hair which he wore in a pony-tail, or that he sported a large moustache of the type associated in England with RAF pilots. The two men's personalities could hardly have been more different. Douglas was a paragon of caution, guile and understatement, a man whose way of praising something was to list the various defects and drawbacks it didn't have. Raymond, on the other hand, splashed out recklessly on terms like 'fabulous', 'unbelievable' and 'amazing', which thrifty Douglas saved for occasions so special that in practice they never occurred. By turns vivacious, lethargic, sentimental, mordant, vulgar, rhetorical, tolerant, selfish, wise and superficial, he seemed remarkably unspoiled by the knowledge that he could get away with anything. Even those who couldn't stand him in principle found his charm irresistible in person.

Aileen's social life lifted off like a rocket. Raymond possessed the most extraordinary facility for making friends, and by British student standards he seemed to have plenty of money. Aileen was not surprised by this, casually taking it for granted that all American parents were rich and generous. Where Douglas had taken her for wet walks along the coast, Raymond arranged a trip on a fishing boat whose skipper he'd got to know. He bought a motorbike and took Aileen over to France for weekend excursions. On her nineteenth birthday they drove to a small airfield outside Brighton, where a friend with a pilot's licence loaded them both into a small plane and flew low over the roofs of the city for an hour while Raymond urged him to ever more daring exploits. Afterwards Aileen was trembling so much he had to carry her to the car. 'You think *I* wasn't scared too?' he told her. 'I was shitting bricks, man! But let me just ask you one thing. Are you ever going to forget today? No way, right? That's what it's all about!' There was a darker side to this spontaneity, too. Raymond would disappear from Brighton for days on end without the slightest notice. Aileen's attempts to make him feel guilty about this brought out his most irritating vein of cracker-barrel philosophizing. 'Hang loose,' she was told. 'Go with the flow. Don't fight your karma. If you love me, set me free.' Nor was it the slightest use trying to find out where he went or what he did on these trips. It was not that he seemed secretive, merely that his total dedication to the present moment – 'the only one we ever actually live, here and now, where it always is' – precluded any interest in what had happened yesterday. When he was away, he ceased to exist; the moment he returned, their relationship resumed with undiminished intensity. So Aileen was not unduly surprised when she arrived back at their Kemp Town flat one winter afternoon to find Raymond packing. 'I've got to go,' he told her. 'It's my mom. She's ill, like really. I just got a call.' That evening they took a train to Gatwick. Raymond bought a ticket on the first flight out, to Amsterdam, where he could get a connection to Los Angeles. He promised to phone regularly, gave her a number to call, and estimated that he would be back in a week at most. After seventy-two hours without news, she rang the number he had given her and discovered that it was 'inoperative'. Seventeen days later a wrinkled aerogramme arrived, informing her that he had decided to stay on 'for a while'. In terms whose extreme vagueness seemed almost insulting, he described a life of mild indolence. There was no reference to his mother's health.

The following period of her life was the worst Aileen had ever known. The pain was so dreadful, so real, that she was worried it might be doing her some permanent injury. Sometimes she would survey her body in the mirror, astonished that it was all there. She looked pale, strained, emptied, stripped of the beauty that Raymond had lovingly discovered and cultivated. She wrote shameless letters, holding nothing back, not trying to be clever. The few he wrote in reply were brief and superficial, but she forgave him that, knowing that no sane person could *choose* to feel the intensity of emotion which had been visited upon her. She had decided that the moment she completed her degree she would go to him, and in the meantime she immersed herself in bureaucratic details: arranging for visas, applying for the graduate programme at UCLA, studying for her final exams. She arrived in California in late June, having received a first-class degree almost without noticing. Raymond appeared at the airport an hour late. In his native environment, he seemed a different creature: slighter, quieter, dowdier, poorer and less exotic. More alarmingly, he didn't seem particularly glad to see her. They drove a long way through an unvarying suburban landscape to a rickety wooden house on a block zoned for redevelopment which he shared with a group of other 'heads'. The mood was downbeat, the vibes bad. Most of Raymond's former friends were either in Vietnam or exiled to Canada or Mexico. He himself had successfully avoided the draft before going to Europe, by volunteering for immediate action on the grounds that he liked killing people and couldn't wait to begin. But the recruiting boards had wised up since then and the local drop-out community had been decimated. Every evening the television news sprayed scenes of carnage over the walls of the doomed head-house, and all the occupants' jokes about the footage being mocked up on a back lot down the road at Burbank, like the famous moon walk, didn't really help. The sixties were over, things had changed, the feeling had gone. In an attempt to bring it back, Raymond and his friends continually upped their consumption of speed, mescaline and acid.

This created problems for Aileen. In Brighton she had been quite prepared to smoke a little grass or hash from time to time, but she had always drawn the line at harder stuff. But on the West Coast, this attitude was labelled 'up-tight'. 'If you don't try it, how do you know you don't like it?' was Raymond's argument. To him this seemed unanswerable, and Aileen was feeling so insecure that she didn't dare refuse. So one evening, alone with him in their attic bedroom, she dutifully took communion, placing a thin rectangle of acid-soaked blotting paper on the tip of her tongue. She was ready for monsters or miracles. What actually happened was, on the face of it, less dramatic. Ever since her childhood, Aileen had had a recurring dream. She called it her 'flying dream', although the actual sensation involved was more like floating than flying. There was more to it than that – a specific time and place, a certain landscape – but all she could ever remember afterwards was the sensation of smooth fluid motion, of gliding about, hovering weightlessly an inch or two above the ground, able to move in any direction without the slightest effort or resistance. What happened the first time Aileen dropped acid was that she entered the dream again, but as a conscious participant. Afterwards she remembered no more than on her previous visits, but she was able to reconstruct something of the scenario from Raymond's teasing account of her antics. 'It was like you were some kind of guide showing people around a stately home or something. You kept pointing out the highlights of the place and making all these cracks about American tourists, like I was some kind of red-neck on a package tour. "Just look at that lawn!" you told me. "You don't have grass like that in the States. That's something you can't buy with money. Hundreds of years rolling and mowing went to make that lawn. Isn't it lucky my feet don't touch the ground or my footprints would spoil it all." Oh, boy! You were really flying!' He didn't tell her that she had later become hysterical and started screaming about someone falling to his death, and then tried to struggle to the window, and how he'd had to call the others and they'd forced orange juice laced with barbiturates down her throat until she calmed down. She found that out later, after her second trip, from one of the others. At the time she was too relieved to have got her hallucinogenic initiation over successfully to wonder why Raymond never encouraged her to repeat the experience.

Summer turned to winter almost unnoticed in the homogenized climate. Aileen's application for a postgraduate place at UCLA came to nothing, but she wasn't unduly disappointed, having realized by then that her reasons for wanting to study psychology had had little or nothing to do with wanting to be a psychologist. Coupled with this insight was the realization of what she *did* want, what would cure her insecurity, clarify the rather ambiguous situation and make Raymond fully hers at one stroke. In very much the same way that she had decided one night to take Douglas Macklin to bed, Aileen now allowed herself to get pregnant. Even when she was sure that this had been achieved, she did not tell Raymond, although she was only superficially anxious about his reaction. The future was assured; there would be life. The details would arrange themselves somehow.

They did. A few weeks later Raymond went hang-gliding off the cliffs near Santa Barbara, high as a kite on amphetamines. The wind proved too fast for him and tossed his sail into an irreversible spin. At the funeral service one of his friends read a passage from *Jonathan Livingstone Seagull* and concluded that Ray had gone out the best way he knew how. Aileen was presented to Raymond's father, a fundamentalist farmer from the Mid-West who had evidently written off his son as a bad job years before. His wife, it turned out, had died in childbirth a decade earlier. Grief was tossed from hand to hand like a live grenade. Aileen was left to carry it home with her, and she was cradling it to her body, up in the attic room she and Raymond had shared, when it finally went off. She opened the cupboard containing Raymond's stash. Slowly and methodically, as though performing some exacting ritual, she snipped the sheets of acid-soaked blotting-paper into one-inch squares. Then she ate them, one by one.

The next forty-eight hours of her life went missing as completely as a passage erased from a tape. When it resumed, she found herself lying in bed, her whole body a dull ache. It was warm and quiet and still. Figures in white coats came and went, murmuring about miracles. Aileen was beginning to think that her Sunday School teacher's account of heaven must have been correct after all when two of Raymond's friends appeared at her bedside. They explained that when they first saw her lying on the lawn they'd just freaked out and how at first the ambulance pigs wouldn't take her because it didn't look like they had the bread but fortunately Beth was holding because her connection was out of town so she hadn't been able to score. 'You must have been just like totally relaxed,' the girl told her. 'I read about a baby once, it fell like from a fourth-floor balcony into the parking lot and survived. That's because babies are so naturally relaxed. It's only like later on that we get screwed up and have to do yoga and stuff.' The doctors and nurses confirmed that she was lucky to be alive. As for having escaped without fractures or internal injuries of any kind, just superficial abrasions and bruising, well, it was nothing short of a miracle. 'It must be thirty feet from that window to the front yard,' one of them remarked in a tone of near disgust, as though Aileen were a notorious criminal who had been acquitted on a technicality.

A few days later she came home in a taxi to find the house fenced off behind corrugated iron sheeting marked with the name of the demolition company whose bulldozers were already at work scouring the garden. When Aileen glanced up at the attic window, still propped open on its curled stay of wrought-iron, a cry sounded quite distinctly through the rumbling turbulence of the machinery: high, piercing, long drawn out. It was the cry of a baby in distress. Only then did Aileen realize that she had not escaped without loss after all, that a transaction had taken place, that her life had been bought at the cost of another.

The ousted hippie community had temporarily reformed in a flat a few blocks away, and it was there, over the course of the following week, that the final act of Aileen's pregnancy took place. The physical effects were scarcely more painful or dramatic than a very heavy period, but the grief was beyond anything she had ever imagined. She wept almost continuously for days. There was nothing to say, and in any case no one she could have said it to. No one knew that she was mourning not one person, but three: Raymond, their child, and herself. For although she had survived, Aileen knew that from now on she would always be a survivor, someone who was alive *nevertheless*. As soon as she had recovered sufficiently, she wound up her affairs. After settling her hospital bill, she had just enough for a standby ticket to London. Her first reaction on returning was one of astonishment that the place was still there. Although she had been in California for less than a year, its apocalyptic rhetoric had affected her so deeply that she could hardly believe her eyes when she found Britain still going about its seedy unglamorous business, as unimpressed by prophecies of global doom as it had been by the auguries of a new Aquarian age. Aileen literally found herself back where she had started, with nothing to show for her year abroad but a hole in her c.v. and a circle of friends whom she had alienated by either ignoring or patronizing them while she and Raymond had been flying high together. She spent the rest of that year picking up the pieces. First and foremost she needed a job. The best chance of finding one seemed to be in clinical psychology, and with a little help from her former tutor she obtained a place in the MSc course at the Institute of Psychiatry. One of her classes involved travelling to Bloomsbury in order to gain ward experience at the National Hospital for Nervous Diseases in Queen Square. She was aware that part of the hospital building was occupied by the Institute of Neurology, but her whole life before Raymond now seemed so unreachably distant that when a tall sandy-haired man stopped her in the corridor one day and identified himself as Douglas Macklin, she felt as though destiny must have brought them together.

If Britain had seemed reassuringly unchanged, Douglas was the very core of that immutability. 'So how was America?' he inquired as casually as though he were asking her about a film she'd been to see. In another context – after fifteen years of marriage, for instance – this remark might well have struck Aileen as insufferably crass. At that moment it was just what she wanted to hear. With a shrewdness new to her, she scanned Douglas's appearance and manner for signs of a female presence in his life. She failed to find any. He invited her up to his place for dinner later that week. Aileen didn't stay the night, but they agreed to meet again and on that occasion she did. Douglas's love-making, as clumsily well-intentioned as ever, sealed her sense of security. Here was no giddy spinner, no flighty drifter who dreamed of staying high for ever. Douglas Macklin was real, solid and comfortingly inadequate. She knew she could manage him. When she proposed that they get married, he frowned slightly, and then said, 'I can't see any reason why not.'

A decade and a half later, Aileen could see plenty. Her husband's work on neuroendocrinology had been rewarded with a research fellowship, but the major breakthrough which he had hoped would establish his name internationally had failed to materialize. After finishing her postgraduate course, Aileen had spent some time at Maudsley Hospital, specializing in the problems of young people. She now worked in the Adolescent Unit of a psychiatric hospital not far from the Macklins' home in a large Edwardian house in Stamford Brook. For reasons which Aileen thought she understood too well to want to verify, the marriage had remained childless. The couple's days were devoted to work; their nights, with rare exceptions, to sleep. As soon as she got home, Aileen went up to her study, where she read or listened to the radio or just stared out of the window until it was time to prepare the evening meal. Meanwhile, in the living room, Douglas drank several glasses of whisky cut with progressively less water and watched the news, first on ITV, then on BBC1, and finally on Channel 4. At eight o'clock husband and wife met across the dinner table and battle commenced.

Aileen could no longer remember at what point she had perceived the basic mechanism, so startling in its simplicity: their marriage was a closed system with only a limited amount of any given emotion available. It followed that if one of them had more, the other must have less. For example, if Douglas came home from work elated by some success, Aileen immediately began to feel depressed. If, on the other hand, something had made him tense and snappy, she at once became more confident and relaxed. It worked the other way too, of course. Her good news depressed him, her failures gave him heart. Consciously or not, Douglas was aware of this too, hence the battle. Although the quantity of emotion involved in these exchanges was quite small, it was often critical, just sufficient to make or break the evening for either partner. Moreover, since appearance was all, one could easily cheat. If Douglas could convince her that he was calm and serene, Aileen began to feel tense and edgy, which in turn induced a real calmness and serenity in him. Deceit had become reality; the fake had verified itself.

She could play the game too, but unfortunately she had made two fatal errors. One had been years before, back in their student days at Sussex. Late one evening, in the course of a rambling account of why she was studying psychology, Aileen had mentioned that there was a strain of insanity in her family. She had done this out of vanity: in 1968 madness was still 'interesting'. Besides, she wanted to show off her sophistication, to demonstrate her awareness of her own motives. 'I suppose that studying the subject is a way of coming to terms with the anxiety that I might be tainted myself,' she had told Douglas, 'a way of defusing the whole idea of madness through a process of objectification.' To call it madness had actually been exaggerating wildly. All Aileen knew for sure was that her grandmother had begun behaving rather oddly towards the end of her life, and that when Aileen herself had been a child, her mother claimed to have been worried that Aileen might have inherited this 'oddness'. Exactly what had happened to justify this remained unclear. As far as Aileen had been able to gather later, it amounted to nothing very much more than a tendency to sleepwalk during the periods of insomnia from which she suffered around the time of the full moon. At all events, she had quite forgotten having mentioned the matter to Douglas until the occasion of her second mistake, which was to try to discuss openly with him the deteriorating state of their marriage. To her dismay, her husband had not only refused to talk about it, but had rejected her description of the situation as distorted and exaggerated. 'If you don't mind me saying so,' he replied in that solicitous tone which she had come to fear and loathe, 'I think you read a good deal too much into things. When I come home in the evening I'm far too exhausted to have any interest in playing the kind of games you're talking about. I just want to rest, to relax and chat like a normal couple. You don't suppose there's any danger of you becoming too involved in your work, do you, Aileen? It's always bound to be a risk, I should imagine. Particularly for someone with your background.' It was only then that Aileen remembered having told him about the 'madness' in her family, and realized with despair that she had handed her husband a weapon which would assure him of victory any time he chose to use it.

Douglas Macklin poured the last of the wine into his glass and inspected the little flurry of sediment with a passionately disinterested eye. Without this expression changing in the slightest, he transferred his gaze to his wife.

'So this boy,' he said. 'Gary, is it? I didn't quite catch your conclusion. It almost sounds as though you think he might be right, that someone really is trying to kill him.'

Aileen lit the cigarette for which her husband had made her wait while he toyed with the remnants of his meal.

'Someone's trying to kill all of us.'

'Really? How thrilling. Who, for instance?'

'You watch the news, don't you? The PLO, the IRA, the multinational drug companies, the nuclear-generating people. There are enough missiles targeted on London to kill everyone a hundred times over, or is it a thousand?'

The scatty female role was one of her more successful defences, no doubt because Douglas's residual sexism made it difficult for him to accept that it wasn't genuine.

'Oh, I see!' he exclaimed. 'You mean this lad of yours is just another burned-out *Guardian* reader.'

Aileen gazed at him from behind a deliberate smile.

'And how's your work going?' she asked brightly. Too brightly, in fact, for it revealed that his irony had been wasted on a false target.

'Oh, it's all rather mundane and boring, I'm afraid,' he purred. 'Listening to you, I get quite nostalgic for the old days when the brain seemed to be something special, the seat of magic powers and terrible forces. As usual, reality is less exciting. The brain has turned out to be just another gland, of no more general interest than the kidney or the pancreas. Really, sometimes I almost envy you.'

Aileen carefully flicked ash from the end of her cigarette. Whatever happened, she must not allow herself to be provoked. By the law of compensation, the angrier she became, the cooler her husband would remain. Conversely, if she could frustrate him long enough then he might lose his temper, in which case she would have won.

'Envy me? Because I deal with the whole person, you mean, not just a mass of tissue?'

'No, no. I envy you because you live in the past, professionally speaking. You're treating people whose mental models of the brain were formed years ago, back in the Dark Ages. Your patients are like country folk who still believe that ghosts walk in the woods at night and mutter darkly about strange goings-on at the great house. In fact the woods have all been levelled on an EEC grant and the house is now the headquarters of the local agribusiness, but you're still up to your ears in tall tales about spooks and spirits.'

'My job is to help people get better. I use the most up-to-date methods available.'

'But that's still primitive in terms of current research. Take this boy of yours, for example. From a state-of-the-art perspective, he's simply suffering from an endocrine disorder requiring hormonal analysis and treatment to correct the imbalance. That's a world away from the land where you live, inhabited by demons with names like Schizophrenia and Paranoia. No one has ever seen these demons or knows how their power operates, but everyone believes that they haunt people. Your task, as the local witch-doctor, is to identify the demon that is haunting a given patient and then prescribe the appropriate healing ritual. I know that's the best you can do. We can't yet deliver therapeutically. Fair enough. But the fact remains that the difference between your view of mental life and the one we'll be kicking around in Boston' – Douglas was going to a conference at MIT at the end of the week – 'is like the difference between a modern atlas and one of those old *mappa mundi* consisting of a dodgy outline and lots of blank space inscribed with comments like "Here be monsters." '

Aileen crushed out her cigarette and stood up, stacking their plates together.

'Our cures work,' she said.

'Do they? The last set of figures I saw seemed to be something less than totally conclusive. In any case, witch-doctors don't do so badly either, you know. Never underestimate the placebo effect. At least a third of all people suffering from anything at all will show some improvement on being told, for example, to gargle a mixture of tomato ketchup and hot lemonade last thing at night.'

This was wild enough to be ignored with safety. Recognizing that he had settled for a draw, Aileen pushed her way through to the kitchen and put the plates in the sink to soak. As she turned off the water she caught sight of the woman reflected in the glass. It was the end of September and the nights were starting to draw in rapidly. Aileen had always had a difficult relationship with those regular features of hers, that ovality so prized by the eighteenth-century land-owning class that they paid painters to clamp them on like a mask. The sixties had had very different ideals, and in her youth Aileen had worked hard to look striking and strange. She had learned that perfection is inflexible. The moment she tried to do anything with it, her face turned dumpy, common and ordinary. It was not until she met Raymond that she was able to accept that her features were *herself*, that there was no difference between the person others saw and the person she was. Until then, the most important parts of her body had seemed to be her hands and feet, whose size her mother was always bemoaning, and her eyes, which had traditionally been put forward as her 'strong point'. She had thus grown up with the image of herself as a bug-eyed stick insect with boxing-glove hands, Army-boot feet and nothing to speak of in between. But Raymond told her she had a 'neat ass' and 'cute tits'; Raymond told her he loved her pussy; Raymond told her that she was beautiful. In Cheltenham, 'beautiful' was a word without resonance, applied to a cup of tea or a vase of flowers or the weather.

It indicated that the strictly limited degree of satisfaction which might reasonably be expected from such things had in fact been forthcoming. But when Raymond used it, the word *glowed*. 'You're beautiful,' he told her. 'You're really beautiful.' True, he had also used to joke that with someone so 'typically English and straight' on the pillion, he was always waved through Customs without question on their motorcycle trips across the Channel. But for Aileen his love had abolished the distinction between her private and public selves. When it returned, it was in a subtly different form. For although the image now thrown back by the darkened window reminded Aileen once again of those dead land-owners, it was no longer their fatuous insipidity that she read there, but the emptiness and tragedy of lives given over to externals. Those matching sets of rigid features had been as necessary an artifice as the protective masks doctors had once given soldiers whose faces had been erased by shrapnel.

A sound vibrated through the whole house. Starting somewhere upstairs, it slithered down, a long-drawn-out keening that finally turned over on its side and swirled away like a television picture being put through its paces by computer graphics. Someone less familiar with the house than Aileen might have thought that it was the cry of a baby in distress, but she was well aware that there was no baby in the house and never would be. As for the sound, it came from the water pipes. The mains feed to the storage tank in the attic had burst the previous winter, and the plumber who had come to mend it had allowed an assortment of noises to escape into the system. Aileen stood listening to it fade away, the dishwater already drying on her hands, staring at the woman reflected in the window. She looked deceptively normal. Only in her eyes, perhaps, was there a hint of something missing. She had survived, certainly, thanks to a miracle, but her life was to all intents and purposes over. At thirty-five, Aileen Macklin was absolutely certain that she was a person to whom nothing more would ever happen.

TWO

In fact things were starting to happen at almost exactly that moment, but Aileen was not to know about them until Pam Haynes telephoned her shortly after eight o'clock the following morning.

Aileen was sitting alone at the dining-table, smoking the first of the three cigarettes she allowed herself daily. Except when Douglas cheated her of it by leaving late, this interval between his departure for work and her own was like a second sleep, a moment of stillness and solitude that made everything that followed possible. It was a fine morning. The room was divided in two by a beam of sunlight through which the cigarette smoke unwound in lazy coils. At the extreme upper corner of the window a patch of blue sky was just visible. Aileen therefore felt particularly resentful when the phone went off like an alarm clock.

'It's Mrs Haynes,' announced a breathy female voice. 'I don't know if you remember but I'm Gary Dunn's social worker. I tried calling the Unit but there was no one there who knew about Gary and I found you in the book. I'm at the Assessment Centre, there's been some trouble.'

Aileen listened to the dull thumping of her blood, amplified by the telephone receiver.

'What sort of trouble?'

'You couldn't stop by here, could you? I wouldn't ask except it's actually quite urgent. It's a bit difficult to discuss on the phone the way things are this end, if you know what I mean. It's not far really. Only it's got to be before nine, you see.'

Aileen stubbed out her cigarette in an ashtray decorated with a design showing an eager swain pursuing a coy nymph through a pastoral landscape.

'He's all right, is he?' she said.

'Yes. Well, more or less.'

'Give me the address.'

Outside, the sky was already filling up with cloud. By mid-morning it would be completely overcast. It never happened the other way round, she thought. There was obviously some law at work, one of the many whose effects she observed without ever understanding what had caused them.

The local authority Observation and Assessment Centre for Disturbed Adolescents was situated in Fulham, not far from Putney Bridge. Pamela Haynes had been strictly accurate in saying that it was not far, but in the rush-hour traffic every mile took the best part of ten minutes. Aileen spent the time reviewing what she knew about the case. Pamela Haynes had originally referred Gary to the Unit back in July, claiming that he 'exhibited symptoms of confusion, disorientation and oral hallucinations of a schizophrenic kind'. Doctors value the rare and exotic as much as anyone else, and the prospect of a patient suffering from hallucinations of taste caused a brief flutter of interest, which promptly collapsed when further inquiry revealed that Mrs Haynes had confused 'oral' and 'aural'. What she meant, as she put it in the course of a conversation with the consultant psychiatrist, was that Gary was 'screwed up and hearing things'.

The boy's social history made it clear that there was no shortage of reasons for his problems, whatever they might be. Quite apart from his involvement in the murder, the exact extent of which was still unclear, the seventeen-year-old seemed to be all alone in the world, without a home or a history, friends or family. Bureaucratically he didn't exist. The various agencies concerned with housing and feeding the homeless had no record of a Gary Dunn, and the instances of the name thrown up by official databases all proved to be dead ends. The police lost interest once it became apparent that he wasn't going to tell them anything they didn't already know about the murder. He was taken into care by the local authority's social services department, who assigned him to Pamela Haynes's supervision. After a few weeks she contacted the Adolescent Psychiatric Unit. No one there took the social worker's diagnosis of schizophrenia seriously, but there was no question that the boy did need care and treatment. The consultant's psychiatric assistant, who conducted the initial interview, prescribed a course of anti-depressant drugs and arranged for out-patient treatment consisting of group and occupational therapy.

Aileen's first contact with the boy had been when one of the nurses brought him into the ward sitting room in the middle of her morning open group, a low-key affair providing general supportive counselling. The moment Aileen caught sight of him, she felt as though someone had laid a velvet-gloved hand on her heart: a touch that was soft, gentle, warm, yet almost unbearably intrusive and intimate. There were at least a dozen people in the room, yet she felt utterly isolated. The surroundings seemed to shimmer and tremble as though she were about to faint. Nor would that have been very surprising, given the strength of her conviction that the boy standing in front of her was her dead child.

It lasted only a few moments. Then, as with *déjà vu*, reality closed ranks and blandly asserted that nothing of the sort had happened, that she must have imagined the whole thing. Aileen's new patient was an unremarkable adolescent with the puffy unfinished look of his age, like partially baked dough. His reddish hair was cropped close to the skull in one of the currently fashionable styles that Aileen, who struggled to keep up with these things like someone running after a bus, still associated with conscription or lice. He and the nurse were still only midway across the room, which was how Aileen knew that no more than a few moments had passed.

In the course of this and subsequent encounters, Aileen noted her observations for the boy's file. Apart from a predominantly blank or wary expression, his appearance was fairly normal. His level of education was evidently low to non-existent, although he was intelligent enough. He tended to be shy and withdrawn, never speaking unless spoken to, and then usually only a word or two at a time. It was *what* he said that revealed disturbance. As Aileen was so unwisely to announce to her husband, Gary Dunn had claimed that someone was trying to kill him.

The Unit's standard report form contained a box labelled

'Delusions: systematized/unsystematized', with space below for further details. Aileen ticked 'systematized' and added 'persecution, guilt (?), ideas of reference'. The consultant psychiatrist would decide, but to Aileen none of this seemed schizoid. The hells in which schizophrenics suffer appallingly real torments look from the outside like a montage cobbled together from a variety of no-hope films featuring leaden plots, unconvincing special effects and rotten acting. But Gary's story was simple, straightforward and consistent. 'There's this bloke, the one who did it. He knows I seen him. He's after me. He's going to do me too.' When asked what this man looked like, the boy replied that he walked funny, like he needed to go to the toilet, and smiled a lot, only it wasn't a real smile. Aileen highlighted this in her report. Unlike patients suffering from paranoid schizophrenia, who tend to identify their persecutors with anybody and everybody from one of the cleaners to a television announcer, Gary Dunn apparently had a specific individual in mind. As for the famous aural hallucinations, these proved to consist simply of a voice saying such things as 'You'll be sorry', 'I'll get you', and 'You'll wind up the same way'. This, too, was quite unlike the sadistic ranting or insinuating murmurs to which schizophrenics are subjected. Finally, Aileen noted that there was no inappropriacy of affect. One characteristic of schizophrenia is that emotional cause and effect gets out of synch. Patients laugh indifferently even as they describe in lurid detail the fiendish schemes which they claim are being devised to bring about their downfall. Gary, on the other hand, evidently found it almost intolerably distressing to talk about the supposed threat to his life. More than once, indeed, Aileen felt almost inclined to doubt whether this *was* necessarily a delusion. After all, murder had been done and no arrest had been made. The police had released Gary for lack of evidence, but they still suspected that he'd been involved in some way, and probably knew who had done it. Supposing he did, thought Aileen, and the murderer knew that he knew? Then the boy's life might indeed be in danger.

Paradoxically, the boy himself would have none of this.

'I'm sick,' he told Aileen firmly. 'Sick in the head.'

At first sight this seemed a positive sign. Psychiatric patients display varying degrees of insight into their condition: some stoutly maintain that there is nothing whatever the matter with them, others claim that their symptoms are the side-effects of a purely physical illness; a third group, usually the more hopeful cases, can see that something has gone wrong and that it is connected with what has happened to them in the past. But Gary Dunn did not fit into any of these categories.

'What do you think is the matter with you?' Aileen asked him one day.

'I got schizafreakout, haven't I?'

She repressed a smile.

'What makes you think that?'

He shrugged impatiently, as though the answer was both obvious and unimportant.

'You know when you've got something, don't you? When you're ill.'

'How do you mean, ill?'

'Like a cold and that.'

'You mean that having a cold and having schizophrenia is just the same?'

'Course it's not the same!' he exclaimed indignantly. 'What I got, you get locked up for, right? It's in the head, isn't it? It's dangerous. I might *do* things. There's no telling what I might do.'

And he rolled his eyes as though appalled by the extent of his potential depravities. At the same time Aileen could hardly keep from smiling, but as the weeks passed it became apparent that the boy really meant it. This was a rarity indeed. The staff at the Unit were used to patients who were more or less unwilling to be admitted or unhappy about staying, but few of them had ever come across someone who was positively eager for admission. Gary's hints that he should be 'locked up' gradually turned to demands which grew ever more strident. To bolster his case, he took to aping the behaviour of the other patients, mimicking their tics and fits. Jenny Wilcox, the occupational therapist whose office was next to Aileen's, witnessed one of these demonstrations. 'It was truly awful,' she reported.

'Unbelievably bad. Even brain-damaged yobs like Stan and Trevor could see that he was faking it. We all just sat there and *cringed* for him.' Gary Dunn's exhibitions failed to convince not only Jenny's 'yobs' – her term for the more seriously disturbed male adolescents – but everyone else at the Unit from the consultant down. No one understood why he was so anxious to be admitted, but the fact remained that he was just one of many patients whose needs and wishes had to be taken into account. The pressure on beds was so severe that there could be no question of turning one over to a patient whose condition was not serious enough to warrant it. What worried Aileen as she drove down Fulham Palace Road that Tuesday morning was the thought that there was one sure way that the boy could gain instant admission, did he but know it, and that was by making a suicide attempt.

The Assessment Centre occupied two sprawling turn-of-the-century houses which had been knocked together and extended in various ways to form a shapeless mass burgeoning with odd excrescences. Inside, walls had been swept away and new partitions built, so that it was impossible to reconstruct the original shape or purpose of the rooms. In an attempt to make the place less institutional, these had been named rather than numbered. At one time there had been a rhyme and reason to the names, with 'Mars', 'Venus' and 'Saturn' all on one corridor, for example. But the signs had been defaced by generations of inmates – in this case, to 'Wars', 'Penis' and 'Fatcunt' – so that the layout of the building was as baffling as its external appearance suggested. Aileen had arranged to meet Pamela Haynes in the warden's office, but her attempts to find it led her back again and again to a recreational area where four young men were playing table-football while two others sat in front of the television watching a man in a waxed jacket explain how to grow larger roses. They all turned to stare at Aileen each time she reappeared, and she realized that she was gradually losing caste in their eyes. Revealed as a fake figure of authority, unable to find her way about, she was acutely conscious of being just a woman alone among a pack of young males whose murky feelings for the opposite sex were quite evident from those renamed rooms. So when Pamela Haynes appeared, looking for her, she got a warmer reception than would otherwise have been the case.

The social worker was a gawky woman run aground in her late thirties. Her expression was drained and harassed, with the vampire–victim look of those who spend too much time giving to others and getting little or nothing in return.

'Thanks ever so for coming,' she gushed dully. 'We should just be in time. The office opens at nine, you see, and Leonard, that's the warden, will have to phone in then. He's ever such a decent bloke, but it is a criminal offence, after all. They'll have him charged unless we do something. It gets rid, you see, which is all they think about these days. But after what the poor little bugger's been through already it would just finish him, wouldn't it?'

'What happened?'

'They caught him trying to set fire to some curtains. Last night, it was, about nine o'clock. It wasn't serious, but he'll have to go, of course. The question is where.'

They exchanged glances.

'You want us to take him,' Aileen said.

'It's either that or the police. They'd love a chance to have another go at him. They still think he's holding out about the murder. With this hanging over him, they could give him the works.'

Aileen stared for a while at the floor, which was clad in vinyl tiles of an indeterminate shade.

'Where is he?'

'In the warden's office. That's why I couldn't talk on the phone. He was sitting at my elbow. Do you want to see him?'

'I'd better speak to the warden first.'

Leonard was a thickset man wearing a faded tweed jacket with elbow patches, corduroy trousers worn at the knees, and Hush Puppies, which, like their owner, suffered from premature baldness. He looked like a schoolmaster who is resigned to being a figure of fun to his pupils but hasn't yet realized that his colleagues despise him too. At Aileen's request, he led her upstairs to see where the arson attempt had occurred. The dormitory was a large bare room whose glossy walls and flooring made it seem chilly, although in fact the air was almost suffocatingly close. The curtains had been removed, but the glass panes and the paintwork nearby were tinted more or less darkly with smoke, and the window frame was heavily charred on one side.

'He sprayed the fabric with lighter fuel,' the warden explained. 'Luckily there was an extinguisher just outside in the corridor. 'It's only superficial, you see, the restructuring. If the flames had got at the woodwork underneath the whole issue would have gone up before anyone could have done anything.'

'Who caught him?'

'Well, luckily enough one of the other lads happened to be going to the loo at the end of the corridor. The door here was wide open and as he passed by the curtains went up, whoosh.'

As they walked back downstairs together, Leonard expanded on the difficulties of his situation.

'What it comes down to at the end of the day is that we don't have the staff to cope. Gary's been lucky to have Pam. Most of them are just left to their own devices. We've had sixteen violent assaults on staff members during the last year alone.'

It was only after they entered the warden's office and Aileen saw the boy, his face swollen and discoloured, that she understood why she was being told all this.

'There was nothing I could do,' the warden went on quickly. 'While we were putting out the fire and cleaning up a group of them took him into the toilets. I don't mean to condone violence of course, but, well, you can see their point. I mean, if he'd done it when there was no one around we'd all have ended up like Walls' bangers.'

'But he didn't, did he?' Aileen snapped. 'Didn't any of you have the wit to think of that?'

A rush of helpless love swamped her, an almost overwhelming urge to take the boy in her arms. She observed this lunatic impulse as one might the thought of hurling oneself from the top of a high building, knowing very well that it won't happen but faintly appalled that one has even entertained such an idea. By now Aileen had come to terms with the fact that her relationship with Gary Dunn was characterized by the most powerful case of counter-transference she had ever come across. It is common for patients undergoing psychotherapy to transfer to the therapist the emotions they have felt for earlier figures of authority. Adolescents in particular tend to identify a female therapist with their mothers. Nor is it uncommon for the therapist to experience an equivalent counter-transfer of emotion, and as a childless woman working with young people Aileen had long realized that she was particularly vulnerable to this. But the feelings she experienced for Gary Dunn were of a different order from any she had previously had to cope with. Once the shock of the initial encounter had passed, she had been able to rationalize what had happened to some extent. If her child had survived, it would have been about the same age as Gary. Moreover, there was a fugitive similarity between the boy and Raymond: the hair colour and certain facial expressions in particular. The real problem about the experience was that she couldn't talk about it. Not to Douglas, for obvious reasons, but not to her colleagues either. Jenny Wilcox had been known to argue that the NHS could only carry on because women were so anxious to be indispensable that they were prepared to accept pay and conditions that no other workers would tolerate. But that didn't mean that Aileen could safely air her feelings about Gary Dunn. The medical services might indeed depend on exploiting women's maternal emotions, but they would no more welcome staff who really confused a patient with their unborn child than the Army draft board had welcomed Raymond when he told them he couldn't wait to start killing people.

'I told you!' Gary told Aileen triumphantly as soon as the warden and Mrs Haynes had left them alone together. 'They made me do it, the voices! I've got to do everything they tell me to.'

This shook Aileen.

'What voices?'

'The ones I hear in my head! I told you something would happen if you didn't have me locked up. You'll have to take me now, won't you? There's no saying what they might tell me to do next time.'

'You've never said anything about these voices before.'

She was confident of this. Such controlling voices are one of the textbook symptoms of schizophrenia. If Gary had ever mentioned them, Pamela Haynes's diagnosis would not have been so swiftly dismissed.

'What else do they tell you, these voices?'

'They tell me not to believe what the doctors say, not to trust them. They tell me not to take those pills they gave me. They say I'm no good, useless, evil. They say I should kill myself.'

Aileen sighed. 'We just sat there and *cringed* for him,' Jenny had said of one of Gary's earlier performances. This was almost as embarrassing.

'We can't let you come and live in the Unit if you're going to set fire to things,' she pointed out.

'I won't, not in there.'

'But you said that you had to do whatever the voices tell you. Suppose they tell you to do this again?'

'They won't.'

'How do you know?'

'They just won't!'

Aileen walked over to the window, where an enormous rubber plant ran up to the ceiling and flattened out like a genie from a bottle. She wiped her finger over the surface of one of the leaves, skimming off a film of dust. There was a bed free in one of the admission wards until the weekend. That was only three days, but at least it would keep the boy out of the hands of the police for the moment. There was little risk of another arson attack, she was sure of that. Gary had set fire to the curtains in a carefully premeditated gesture, choosing a room where there was a fire extinguisher handy, leaving the door wide open and then waiting until someone was passing by before actually striking the match.

Without committing herself to anything, Aileen made some reassuring noises and then slipped out to the hallway where the warden and Pamela Haynes were waiting. She told them that she would do what she could to have Gary admitted to the Unit and would be in touch later that morning.

She had left her battered red Mini – a hand-me-down from

Douglas, who had moved up to a Volvo – in the street opposite the Centre. The door of a lock-up garage nearby had been decorated with an assortment of graffiti, including 'Take 2 you shit crew', 'Skin one up', and 'Hip hop don't stop'. But for some reason Aileen's eye was drawn to four words carefully printed one above the other.

EAT
SHIT
DIE
BOX

As she completed her journey to work, Aileen repeated them over and over to herself. She didn't normally take any notice of graffiti, but for some reason she couldn't get those four words out of her mind. It wasn't until the main hospital was in sight that she succeeded in bringing her thoughts to heel. Yes, she would probably be able to let Gary into the Unit until the end of the week, unless the consultant chose to object. Assuming that the boy's idea that someone was trying to kill him was a delusion, then like all delusions it must have been a function. There must be some knowledge that he could not admit he had, some fact from his past which was too traumatic for him to accept. If Aileen was to help him, she would have to discover what this was, and that meant getting behind the boy's defences, probing into his past. For it was there, she was convinced, that the source and explanation of his imaginary terrors lay hidden.

THREE

Eight months before, back in the dead of January, Gary Dunn had been two years younger. His name had been Steve then, Steven Bradley, and he'd been sleeping in a length of concrete tubing under the Westway flyover, between Wood Lane and the underground tracks, until the stotters took him in. They were older, big kids, almost grown-ups. He'd seen them before, the stiff robotic march, the swollen plastic bags clutched in their hands, the eyes glazed like those of the fish heads he sometimes came across, scavenging in bins for his supper. Nevertheless, it was they who'd saved him from the police. One was called Jimmy and the other Dave, and they'd been hauled in following a complaint from a woman they'd called a silly fucking cow because they didn't like the looks she was giving them. The police had duly handed them a bit of harassment in return, but there was nothing much else they could do. Glue is not an illegal substance, and if the purchaser chooses to exploit its hallucinogenic rather than adhesive properties, he is perfectly within his rights to do so. Life, on the other hand, is something you need to be sixteen to consume without adult supervision. Steve couldn't prove he was, so the constabulary thought they had him bang to rights until Jimmy, a plump toughie with curly fair hair and a face like a bent cherub, decided to throw a spanner in the works.

'He's me brother, isn't he?'

'Piss off,' the desk sergeant told him tonelessly.

'He fucking is! He keeps us half-way straight and all. He looks *after* us. We'd be ever so much worse if he wasn't around.'

'We'd be fucking *monsters*!' Dave confirmed. He was tall and skinny and was wearing a torn denim jacket with 'The Cult' inked across the back, calf-length battledress trousers and large black boots. A line of swastika tattoos ran up his neck and cheek and across his shorn scalp like the footprints of some exotic bird.

The sergeant didn't believe a word of this, of course. He knew that the two stotters were just trying to get their own back for the aggro they'd sustained. But he'd been in the game long enough to know that it wasn't worth his while trying to stop them. It was all a question of energy. Despite the horrendous things they did to themselves, these kids had so much, whereas the sergeant, for all his diets and keep-fit and early nights, was still knackered by tea-time. It wasn't fair, youth. Besides, he was just wasting his time with this boy. Ten to one his parents wouldn't want him back, either that or the boy wouldn't go. Social services wouldn't want to know, and as for the charity organizations, if he hadn't stuck with them already it was because he couldn't stand it and would run away again at the first opportunity. In short, it was nothing but a wind-up whichever way you looked at it. The sergeant repeated his previous comment to Jimmy and turned away dismissively.

Outside the police station, Steve started to sidle off.

'*This* way!' Jimmy called, shaking his head scornfully, pulling the boy after him. He proceeded to go on at some length about the mentality of the wankers he was surrounded by, who couldn't even find their way back to the fucking house unless he was there to hold their hands. He soon became so incensed about this that Dave suggested they stop off for a top-up. The filth had taken what they'd had on them – totally illegally, of course, but what were they supposed to do, call their solicitor? – so they dropped into Woolies to restock. A large sign informed customers that the management reserved the right to restrict the sale of solvent-based products, but the cashiers all looked as if they'd been at the stuff themselves and would have checked out a nuclear missile without a second thought as long as it had a price sticker on it. Back in the street, Jimmy pierced the foil membrane sealing the tube and squeezed some glue into the carrier Dave had taken without asking. Then they set out for home, taking turns to clamp the bag to their faces. When Dave had finished he automatically passed the bag to Steve, but Jimmy snatched it angrily away.

'Not little Stevie!' he cried. 'Me mum'd turn in her fucking grave!'

Steve tagged along behind the two stotters, although they appeared to have forgotten about him. He had nowhere else to go.

At the junction of two streets just north of the Uxbridge Road, Jimmy and Dave disappeared. The property at the corner was fenced off by sheets of corrugated iron, and while Steve was standing there uncertainly, an arm suddenly shot out and pulled him through a gap between two of the panels. Inside, it was like being in the country: a rotting meadow of dead grass and spindly weeds. Overgrown shrubs and bushes competed for space and light. The ruined vestiges of steps and a path were clogged with branches, green with mould. Jimmy stuck his pudgy forefinger into Steve's face, just below the boy's eye.

'Count yourself lucky you're not getting a good booting. You get us in trouble with the filth again, I'll fucking kill you.'

If Steve had been sure which panel in the fence opened, he might have tried to make a run for it, but it was too late. Jimmy led the way along a winding path trodden through the matted grass. The house seemed very large, close up like this, in the hushed wilderness inside the fencing. The windows and doors were all boarded up with plywood, but Dave prised back the screen on the back door far enough for them to slip inside. Had the house been for sale, rather than awaiting replacement by a block of retirement flatlets, the estate agents might have described it as 'a rare opportunity to purchase a property offering considerable scope for imaginative refurbishment'. Alex, one of the other residents and good with his hands, had hot-wired the electricity supply, bypassing the meter, and at one time there had been talk of installing heating and even a cooker. But this had come to nothing, and the stairs, doors and skirting-boards, as well as much of the flooring, had been broken up for firewood. On the retreating island of intact floorboards, a number of mattresses lay scattered around a television and video recorder. These had been donated by a contact of Jimmy's who occasionally needed help in enforcing his various business interests. Unfortunately he had ended up on the wrong end of a knife just before Christmas, since when things had been a bit tight.

When Steve and the others came in, Alex was flat out on one mattress watching TV. A girl with white hair and black lips, wearing a lime-green T-shirt, a short silvery skirt, zebra-stripe tights and pink socks, was lying on her belly on another mattress, listening to a Sony Walkman. Her legs were raised behind her and her left foot idly caressed the curve of her right calf. Her name was Tracy, and both she and Alex, a runty street urchin from Belfast, seemed mildly puzzled at first by Steve's presence. But Jimmy was in charge – no one disputed that, except Dave when he had one of his turns – and like the glue itself, his fantasy proved stronger than the reality to which it was attached. Once the Woolworth's bag had circulated a few times, no one except Steve himself had the slightest doubt that he was Jimmy's younger brother and that he lived there with them, looking after them, keeping them half-way straight.

Steve soon settled into the role in which he'd been cast. For the first time in his life – well, the first that bore thinking about, anyway – he filled a gap, completed a family, *belonged*. He went to the shop further down Trencham Road marked OOD S ORE. This satisfied most of the stotters' needs, consisting as it did of a grocery and off-licence which also hired videos. He reminded them when it was time to go and sign on at the DHSS, and then trekked to a distant block of council flats early in the morning to extract the cheques from the broken letter-box which they used as a convenience address. He did his best to keep them from electrocuting or poisoning themselves when they were completely out of it, which was all of every evening and most of most days. Their mediator, their go-between, their *shabbes goy*, he ran errands between them and reality.

Faithful to the letter of Jimmy's scenario, the stotters never allowed Steve to take part in their rituals. He remained a spectator as they inhaled the muddling vapours and passed the plastic cylinders of cider from hand to hand. He watched them gibber and gesticulate, their faces distorted with terror or stupefaction. He watched them fight, usually with clumsy harmless blows that whirled astray, although one night Dave got Jimmy by the throat and squeezed and squeezed with those gristly hands of his until Alex pulled a burning plank from the fire and smashed him over the head with it. He watched them fuck, mounting Tracy one after another with expressions which suggested that the activity was a tedious necessity not unlike defecation. Afterwards they fell asleep where they lay, then got up next day and did it all over again. It was like sharing a cage with a pack of grouchy wild animals, violent and unpredictable, but not too bright. Steve was well aware of the risks he was running, but he reckoned that he could probably keep one step ahead, sensing the stotters' mood shifts before they were aware of them themselves. All in all, he was better off than he had been for a very long time.

Not that his memories went very far back, or were especially detailed. All he had was a selection of images as unconnected and apparently inconsequential as a handful of snapshots. As usual in photographs, everyone was smiling, but Steve didn't make the common mistake of concluding from this that the past was a happy place. The camera often seemed to have been badly aimed, missing the main action, whatever that might have been, to focus instead on the leg of a chair, a section of carpet, or an electric fire with a gleaming concave back which reflected two elements, the lower of which sometimes glowed dully red. When people appeared in the photographs, it seemed to be by accident, as if they'd blundered in unexpectedly, so that only some odd bit of them – a shoulder, part of a dress, a length of hair – emerged clearly. Despite this, Steve was quite content with his memories, even though the crucial one, which would account for the existence of the collection and explain why it was in his possession, was missing.

The finer points of Steve's relationship with his past were, however, lost on Jimmy, who couldn't understand why he didn't just go down the fucking DHSS like everyone else. What did he think he was, some sort of *special* wanker? After the boy had been living there for a few weeks, he and Dave dragged him down to the offices with them, but as soon as Steve saw the row of cubicles where people sat being quizzed by officials he bolted. It was as bad as the police.

That evening things came to a head.

'Look at this muck!' Jimmy exclaimed suddenly. He pointed to the stotters' dinner, consisting of a pack of chicken loaf slices, a packet of crackers and the remains of a tin of cold rice pudding. 'Make you sick! *And* it's fucking near all gone.'

'You know how they make this?' Dave said, holding up the last slice of pale grey meat. 'First they cut their heads off, then they chuck them in this acid bath, burns off all the feathers and that. Then they hose them down, cut them open, yoik out the guts and chuck them in this fucking great press which crushes them, bones and all . . .'

Jimmy turned accusingly to Steve.

'You been stuffing yourself, haven't you? We go out to sign on and you eat all the fucking food in the house!'

'To each according to his ability and from each according to his need,' muttered Alex.

Tracy looked up from painting her fingernails a penetrating shade of purple.

'I'd do anything for a hamburger and chips,' she murmured wistfully.

'What a bunch of wankers!' Jimmy exploded, pounding the floor. 'Never take a single thought for the future, do you? Look at this place! What a dump! *And* they're going to come and tear it down any day now. And what do you do about it? Bring this useless young prick home!'

He pointed at Steve. The others turned to look at the boy as if seeing him for the first time.

'But I thought he's, like, your brother, isn't he?' Dave frowned.

Jimmy gazed at him incredulously.

'My brother! He's not my brother! He's nothing like my brother. I haven't even *got* a fucking brother!'

Dave's frown deepened.

'You mean he's been pissing us about all this time? Oh well, that's, fuck, that's, I mean one thing I can't stand is, I mean you can come up to me, face to face, man to man, and say anything you like . . .'

'Any fucking thing you like,' Alex echoed.

'. . . and if I don't like it then I'll fucking do you, right? But one thing I can't stand is people, people pissing me around, no really, that's the one thing, I mean, that's . . .'

Dave's voice mumbled to a standstill.

'We can't let him go now,' Jimmy mused. 'He knows too much.'

'No one leaves the organization alive,' Alex said in his Ulster accent, as thick and bitter as a gob of phlegm. 'If you're not for us, you're against us.'

'You know the free papers?' Steve said.

Jimmy glared at him.

'Which three papers?' he demanded suspiciously.

'They need people to deliver them. They'll take anyone. It doesn't pay much, but it would be something, for now.'

They all sat staring at the boy for a long time. At last Jimmy nodded slowly.

'Worth a try.'

After that everyone relaxed again. Dave put on the new video, about a disfigured ghoul which tracked down everyone who had ever lived in a certain house and killed them in a variety of colourful ways. As usual, there were wanky patches where character was established and plot developed, and during these Steve's idea gradually took off. By midnight, Jimmy had mapped out a scheme for establishing a distribution empire monopolizing the delivery of free newspapers throughout the country, the work being farmed out to an army of underpaid kids while the real money came straight to him.

'Anyone who wants their fucking newspaper delivered, we're the boys they'll have to talk to!' he enthused, finger stabbing the air to emphasize his point. 'We can name our price! We'll have the whole of England under our thumb!'

'What about Ulster?' Alex put in. 'We gave our blood at the Somme too, you know.'

But his comment was lost in the shrieks of a young woman who was being spectacularly dismembered by the video ghoul.

As is their wont, things looked rather different the next morning. It was Tracy who brought the matter up again. She had a bone to pick with Jimmy, who had urinated in her mouth while she was trying to fellate him the night before. She relieved her feelings somewhat with a number of sarky remarks about the future empire builder, who was slumped in front of the TV watching *Play School*. Sensing a storm brewing, Steve said he would go and phone the *Capital Advertiser*. He returned with the news that there were no distribution vacancies available, which appeared to put paid to that idea. But Jimmy now felt that his credibility was at stake, and so the following Friday the two old-age pensioners who delivered the *Advertiser* to homes in the area were set upon and beaten up and the pram containing their stock of papers dumped off a railway bridge. When Steve phoned again he was told that a vacancy had unexpectedly become available.

Since it was a double round, Alex volunteered to help out. Unfortunately, the only way Alex could face the work was by getting fucked up first, and after he did, one house looked much the same as another. The result was that the residents of one street were each treated to over forty copies of the *Advertiser* dropping through their letter-boxes at five-minute intervals. Some of them phoned to complain, and Alex's brief career in newspaper distribution came to an end. Steve was transferred to another round, further away but short enough for him to do alone. His only worry was that the money had turned out to be so rubbishy – less than a penny per paper – that it wouldn't be enough to keep Jimmy satisfied. Jimmy, however, had more important things on his mind. One of the OAPs he and Dave had put the frighteners on had cashed a couple of pension cheques earlier in the day and was carrying over seventy quid. Jimmy was so impressed by this that he forgot all about Steve's contributions to the housekeeping. Doors were opening up, possibilities beckoning, a whole new lifestyle awaited. Unlike the clueless wankers he lived with, Jimmy had always known that there was more to life than glue and cider and condemned houses. There was heroin and Bacardi and B and Bs on the south coast, to say nothing of souped-up BMWs, designer threads and 250-watt-per-channel stereo rigs. All you needed was cash. Getting it had turned out to be a lot easier than he had imagined.

Meanwhile, Steve carried on distributing the *Capital Advertiser* to 230 homes every week. He liked the job. He saw himself as a sort of postman. He himself never received any post, of course, but he knew that people looked forward to the postman's visits. In a way Steve was even more welcome. The postman brings bad news as well as good, but the bad news Steve brought always happened to other people. There was a lot of it – brave kiddies, tragic mums, heartless conmen, abandoned pets, ravished grannies and torched tramps – but since it all happened to other people, it was actually good news, Steve reckoned. The more bad things happened to other people, the less likely they were to happen to you. Like a postman, Steve had little contact with his clients. As the weeks passed, however, he got to know his route, and came to notice the difference in the doors through which he delivered the paper. They were all roughly the same size and shape, but the closer you looked, the more you realized that each was an individual. A few had clear glass panels, so that you could see right into the hallway, but this was rare, and anyway the hallway was usually so carefully cleaned and tidied that it amounted to another door. The real house – messy, intimate, full of secrets – began further on. More common were panels of frosted glass. Sometimes the glass was only slightly cloudy, with vertical streaks that were almost clear, through which you could catch glimpses of the interior. Steve never saw anything very interesting going on, but he approached these doors with special excitement, for you never knew. But mostly the glass was completely opaque, giving the door an air of false sincerity, like someone making a show of having nothing to hide. Steve preferred the solid wooden doors that shut you out and made no bones about it. They ranged from drab plywood slabs to complex layered jobs with an antique air. Most conformed to a type and must have been identical at one time, but wind and rain, scrapes and scratches, coats of paint, numbers, names, knockers and bells – to say nothing of letter-boxes at any level from Steve's shoulder to his foot – combined to make each a distinct presence which the boy gradually came to know. He found his new acquaintances restful and reassuring. Unlike the stotters, they had no moods. Come rain or shine, they were there, lined up in their places, waiting their turn. Steve fed them one after another, taking his time, pacing himself. It all seemed very safe and satisfying, until one day early in March.

Grafton Avenue was towards the end of Steve's round. One side had been swept away to make room for a council estate, but since this formed part of the adjoining delivery zone Steve was conscious of it only as scenery. His side of Grafton Avenue started off as a terrace of three-storey semi-detached houses with pillared bay windows and steps leading up to an imposing portico where he left a pile of papers, one for each of the flats into which the houses had been divided. Further along these gave way to bijou villas, heavy in architectural extras such as moulded cornices and decorative brickwork. They reminded Steve of the elderly Asian who ran the OOD S ORE: at once plain and exotic, other-worldly and grasping, like a prince in disguise or a magician fallen on hard times. The last house in the road was quite different from all the others. It was so high and narrow that it looked likely to fall over at any moment. The end walls were windowless expanses of mortar, as though the existing house was a remnant of a much larger building. The main floors were set in a bay, giving the house a thrusting, aggressive air. At first sight there was no way in or out, but in fact a path of quarry tiles led into a lean-to porch at the side of the house. Here a short set of steps continued up to an enclosed area where leaves and litter had collected over the years. Once your eyes adjusted to the gloom, you could just make out the front door, four massive panels of unpainted wood separated by strips of heavy scrolling. A large, dull, brass letter-box was inset in the horizontal strip between the upper and lower panels. On the doorpost, at about the same level, was an ivory bell-push in a circular brass surround.

Steve had learned that letter-boxes were as individual as the doors themselves. Some opened as flaccidly as a toothless mouth, others clamped their jaws on the rolled newspaper like playful dogs. But what happened that afternoon in Grafton Avenue was something Steve had never seen before: when he inserted the folded copy of the *Capital Advertiser* into the letter-box, instead of either lying there, wedged and inert, or falling limply through, the paper was plucked from his fingers and pulled smoothly inside, like a video-tape when you put it into the machine.

Steve snatched his hand away before the door had that too. After a moment, the letter-box opened again and an envelope emerged. It tipped over the rim and fluttered to the doorstep as the letter-box closed with a definitive bang. Steve picked up the envelope and ran down the steps and along the path as fast as he could go. Safe in the street again, he set down his orange sling and looked at the envelope. There was no name or address written on it. He tore it open. Inside there was a five-pound note and a pencilled list.

Tin corned beef (Fray Bentos or other reliable brand)
Dried peas
Small pot sardine and tomato paste
Marmite (Large size)
Jam, strawberry for preference
Sugar cubes
Two tins of prunes
Packet of tea
Please leave by door. Keep change.

Steve felt slightly disappointed. He had been hoping for something less ordinary. But when he had finished his round, he went to the Tesco nearby, bought the items on the list and carried them back to Grafton Avenue. When he had almost reached the house again, he noticed a man striding purposefully towards him. He was young, with sharp angular features, all glistening planes of sweaty skin and greasy hair. His face was split in two by a grin like an unhealed wound and his eyes glittered fiercely. His clothes were filthy and threadbare. The trousers were ridiculously short and his socks did not match.

'Do you know what time it is?' he demanded as he reached Steve, who shook his head. The man laughed contemptuously and walked on.

When he reached the house, the boy stood in the street staring at it for a long time. The curtains were all tightly closed and no light showed in any of the rooms. Finally he took a deep breath and scampered rapidly up the path, into the dry sheltered darkness of the porch. He climbed the steps, set the bag down and ran quickly back to the street. He stood and watched for some time, but no one emerged. There was no sound, no movement. The house might have been empty for years. After a while it came on to a drizzle, and Steve turned up his collar and started to walk home through the darkening streets.

FOUR

Whatever the stotters' other shortcomings, a morbid sensitivity to each others' moods was not among them. Steve was perhaps told to stop wanking about rather more often than usual during the week that followed, but the nearest that anyone came to asking him to account for his behaviour was when Jimmy demanded, 'You been at the glue or what?' They were sitting around on what remained of the living-room floor, trying to eat the pizza which Tracy had lifted down Tesco's, not realizing that it only looked like on the cover after being baked in an oven. A few rounds of paint thinner had dulled their disappointment, however, and most of Jimmy's brain was now locked up in the kind of circular activity which will paralyse a computer asked to calculate the square root of minus one. Jimmy's thoughts were less abstruse – he was trying to decide between the relative merits of an indoor or outdoor jacuzzi for the Spanish villa from which he planned to mastermind the drug-smuggling operation he was going to set up as soon as he'd solved his immediate cash-flow problems – but they overloaded his brain so effectively that the mechanism which normally handles swallowing suddenly cut out, leaving Jimmy with a throat full of half-chewed dough going nowhere. Which was all to the good from Steve's point of view, because by the time Jimmy had stopped choking on curses and gobs of uncooked pizza and Alex had observed darkly that it wasn't the coughing that carried you off but the coffin they carried you off in, the boy's state of mind and its causes had been completely forgotten.

In a sense, though, Jimmy's guess had not been so far from the truth. Steve *was* right out of it that week, though this was not down to secret Evostik binges but the prospect of what would happen when he returned to the house in Grafton Avenue the following Friday. The future is a drug to which most people have developed such a tolerance that it requires some quite massive event looming up for their everyday life to be seriously affected, but Steve had spent his fifteen years in a shadowless present where the sun stood always at midday. Now, for the first time, he had something to look forward to, and the effect on his life was like atmospheric lighting in a film: a powerful lateral glare throwing up dramatic shadows, making the ordinary seem strange and exciting. He asked himself the same questions again and again. Who had written the note? Why hadn't he shown himself? Why had he trusted Steve with the fiver? Why couldn't he do his own shopping? At first Steve had thought he might be a cripple or an invalid, but in that case surely he'd be fixed up with the council or whoever it was kept people going till they died. Had he just had an accident, fallen downstairs or something? But in that case why hadn't he asked for help? If Steve hadn't had to go back there the following week he would probably just have forgotten it. As it was, he spent the time wondering and fearing, scheming and dreaming, savouring the bizarre certainty that in a few days he would know the answer.

That Friday was blustery and wet. The protective outer layer of papers was already soaked before Steve could free the cord tying them together and get them into the waterproof orange sling. He had made himself a primitive cape out of a piece of plastic sheeting he'd found in a skip, but the sharp edges scratched his chilled skin and the wind tossed it around so much that it was useless, and he soon threw it away. To keep warm, and in anticipation, he moved briskly from house to house. By the time he turned into Grafton Avenue the street-lamps were beginning to glow very faintly, a deep pinkish shade quite unlike the umber glare that showed once the darkness had firmed up. Steve made short work of the three-storey semis, running up the flights of steps and dumping a pile of papers headlined 'Brave Little Gary Loses His Fight For Life'. The bijou villas got equally short shrift that day, at least until Steve reached the last pair. There he abruptly slowed down, dragging his heels and taking an exaggerated amount of care over the detailed folding and insertion of the paper, for now that he could see his destination it seemed much too near.

The house looked neither more nor less strange than before; an outcast, a relic, a misconception. Despite his delaying tactics, it was no time at all before Steve stood at the wrought-iron gate, in whose bars a potato crisp packet was trapped by the wind like rubbish in a weir. Somewhere nearby an empty beer can rattled noisily about in the gutter. Steve set off up the path of small tiles that curved past an anonymous shrub to the covered entrance where the steps began. Inside, in the hushed darkness, it already felt warmer. Steve climbed the steps one by one, making as little noise as he could. He felt as though anything at all might happen in the next few moments. It was therefore a slight disappointment as well as a relief when nothing did. The folded newspaper he placed in the letter-box just lay there. He pushed it all the way through and heard it flutter to the floor inside. The letter-box snapped shut again. That was all. He turned away, feeling tricked and cheated. Could he have imagined the incident a week before? Sometimes it was hard to tell where his dreams ended and his life began, what had really happened to him and what had occurred in one of those gaps where the normal rules are suspended and someone you think is asleep turns out to be dead on the bed in front of you, in the room you can't get out of no matter how hard you try.

Behind him there was a jarring shudder, as though the whole wall had opened. When he turned, a faint line of light was visible at the edge of the front door. Steve could just make out a figure standing inside. Something white appeared in the opening, fluttering in the darkness like a flag of truce. It was an envelope. Steve reached out and gingerly gripped the corner. The other end was instantly released. He could make out nothing of the figure within except for the eyes, brilliant and restless, busily at work, running over the boy's face and clothing like a pair of scavenging mice, speedy and discreet but missing nothing. Then the door snapped shut. The next moment it looked as though it had not been opened for years.

The list was a lot longer this time, and two five-pound notes were enclosed. It added up to quite a fair weight, too. By now Steve was used to the heavy slingful of papers, but by the time he had finished his round the strap had worn a welt across his shoulder that made it quite painful to carry this additional load, so he decided to stop for a rest. On the way back from the supermarket there was a small park, a triangle of grass intersected by an asphalt path where elderly people stood looking airily around while their panicky-eyed dogs laboured to expel sausage-like turds. Just inside the railings at the entrance to the park was a building providing similar facilities for MEN and OMEN, and Steve had discovered that this was a good place for a rest. You were sheltered from the wind and the rain, and one of the cubicles had a broken window which let in a bit of fresh air to dilute the stink of disinfectant and stale pee. Here Steve would settle down and read through the stories. The walls were covered in them, rambling, repetitive, unpunctuated tales about soiled panties and schoolboys' bums. By now he'd read them all at least once, but knowing what happened and how it all ended just made them more reassuring and relaxing. Surprise, in Steve's experience, was an overrated quality.

When he came out, the wind was stronger than ever. His sodden clothes hung stiffly from his body. He suddenly felt tired and hungry and cold, no longer interested in what was going to happen when he got to the house. He turned into Paxton Grove, the street before Grafton Avenue, and trudged the last few hundred yards to the corner. He was still only half-way up the covered steps when he noticed that the front door of the house was open again. Just a crack at first, but as Steve got nearer the gap started to widen. A wave of warmth reached out and enfolded the boy. There were odours in it, intimate and familiar as the smell of his own body. Half-hidden behind the door was a man wrinkled beyond measure, crumpled and shrunk, fabulously old. His skin was dark and blotchy, ridged and troughed with blood vessels and tendons. Only the eyes looked more or less ordinary, which gave them a freakish, alien appearance in that ruined face, as though he had stolen them.

'Come in,' he urged, beckoning with a hand which resembled one of the bits of chicken that Steve had sometimes found in rubbish bins but learned to reject as inedible. The boy hesitated.

The warmth was still flowing out of the open doorway, as though from a limitless reservoir. Its swirling embrace made him feel light-headed and confused.

'Tea's made,' the old man said.

His eyes never ceased their radar-like sweeps, and in their restless movement Steve read an anxiety even greater than his own. What worried him was the idea that this old man might not really be an old man at all, that once the front door was closed he would start laughing maniacally and then pull off his face and head to reveal the blood-streaked features of the demon beneath, like in Dave's fave video. But there seemed to be no signs that anything of that sort was likely to happen. The man looked no different from any of the other old people Steve had seen making their slow, painful, lonely way along the streets, as though doing penance for some crime. And although he wasn't aware of it, the smells and the warmth of the house were whispering to him all the time, telling him that no harm could come to him there. Hoisting the orange sling with a certain professional flair, the boy stepped over the threshold.

Like the house itself, the hallway was tall and narrow. It was lit by a single bulb enveloped in a large bowl of milky glass, which muffled the light so effectively that Steve could only just make out a flight of stairs reaching up to the invisible ceiling and a door standing open into a large front room whose windows were smothered in velvet curtaining. When the old man had finished locking and bolting the front door, he turned the other way, down a long corridor with brass-handled doors opening off it to either side. The walls were covered in discoloured paper decorated with a design of small flowers in diagonal rows. Floorboards creaked beneath the thin runner of threadbare red carpeting. Steve's fear was still there, but dreamily distanced, like pain by a partial anaesthetic. He had an absurd feeling that they had already walked further than the length of the house. It was no use looking back to correct this illusion, for the old man had already paused to switch off the light behind them.

The corridor came to an end in a cramped alcove with a ceiling that Steve could almost touch. A set of narrow steps ran down to the basement as steeply as a ladder.

'Nearly there,' the old man muttered, starting down.

Steve followed, his dreamlike lack of anxiety still intact. As they descended, it got darker and warmer. At the bottom, Steve actually bumped into the old man, who had stopped, groping for a switch, and this first physical contact between them shocked him almost as much as the time he had touched Tracy's arm accidentally on purpose. Then everything went black as the old man switched off the light at the head of the stairs.

'Bulb's gone down here,' he explained.

Oddly, crazily really, Steve remained unafraid, following the old man forward into a darkness that revealed itself, once he grew used to it, as not quite solid. The leakage of light from somewhere up ahead was just sufficient to reveal the outlines of the old man's figure and the doorways and openings of passages to either side. At last they reached the source of the glimmer, a door standing slightly ajar. Inside, the heat was overpowering. The smells whose tendrils had crept out of the front door were rooted in it, rank and exotic as tropical foliage.

The old man pointed out a large table in the centre of the room. It was draped in a dark red oilskin on which lay a bottle half full of milk, a shiny brown porcelain teapot, a pair of trousers, two chipped mugs with spoons in them, a bag of sugar and a grimy towel. Steve dumped the orange sling on the table and started to unpack the plastic bags of groceries.

'They didn't have Fry's cocoa,' he said.

'Never mind,' the old man said. 'We'll just have to make do, somehow.'

Two drying racks suspended on pulleys from the ceiling supported an assortment of shirts, underclothes and bedlinen, which formed a canopy over the centre of the room. An enormous armchair was drawn up before the cast-iron kitchen range which occupied one entire wall. Both walls and woodwork were covered in thick glossy paint of a creamy yellow shade, the floor in a sheet of dull red linoleum, which was starting to crack and blister and break away from its backing in places.

'And you are?' the old man demanded abruptly.

Steve unpacked a tin of Spam.

'What?'

'What's your name?'
'Steve.'
The old man poured tea into the two mugs.
'Ernest Matthews,' he said. 'How do you like it?'
Steve looked round the room. On the wall opposite stood an enormous sideboard in whose nooks and crannies were lodged shirtstuds, a leadless pencil, stamp edging, several keys, a large seashell, a stuffed weasel, overflowing ashtrays, a magnifying glass, a selection of dried-up fountain pens, buttons, endless scraps of paper, drawing pins, pipecleaners, a cut-throat razor, empty jam jars, coins, pieces of bone, and half a hundred things whose name and purpose, if they had either, Steve did not know. Every single object was covered, as if by protective cotton wool, in a thick even layer of dust. The corner opposite the door was occupied by a bed consisting of a metal frame with a wire mesh to support the mattress. The blankets were thrown back to reveal unclean wrinkled sheets. The pillow still bore the imprint of a sleeping head.
Ernest Matthews glanced at him.
'Eh? Speak up, lad!' he said sharply. 'My ears aren't what they were. How do you like it?'
'It's all right.'
He hoped that this, high praise to the stotters, would do.
'*What*'s all right?' the old man asked with a bemused expression.
Steve shrugged.
'Everything.'
'Well I'm very pleased to hear it, I'm sure!' the old man snapped. 'However, I wasn't asking about everything, I was asking about the tea. How do you like it? Weak? Strong? With or without? Just a dash? One lump or two?'
After a pause, Steve said he didn't know.
'Don't know!' Matthews exclaimed, with a laugh that sounded like a crumpled sheet of plastic film unwrapping itself. 'Well, bless my soul, I'd never thought I'd live to hear a British lad say such a thing.'
He added milk and sugar to both mugs.
'You *are* British, I take it?'

'I can't stay long,' Steve replied.

'Mum and Dad expecting you back, are they? Time for a cup of tea, though. Was there any change from that tenner, by the by?'

Steve laid a handful of coins on the oilcloth. The old man separated fifty pence from the rest.

'That's for you. Have a cake and drink your tea before it stews.'

Matthews took a mug of tea and walked over to the armchair by the stove. When he was settled, he unrolled a tobacco pouch of waxed cloth and started to fill a pipe which he dug out of the creases of the chair.

'You're dripping all over the lino,' he remarked to Steve. 'Haven't you got a proper coat? You'll catch your death, you mark my words.'

Steve sat down on one of the straight-backed dining chairs drawn up to the table and started to sip his tea. Meanwhile the old man took a large brass lighter from another crevice of the armchair and produced a flame of impressive dimensions with which he proceeded to scorch the uppermost layer of tobacco in his pipe.

'Hot in here,' Steve ventured, to break the silence.

Ernest Matthews nodded.

'And do you know the beauty of it? *They don't have to come in the house*. There's a coal-hole round the side, drops straight down into a bunker next door to the scullery.'

He turned his attention to his pipe again. Between puffs the smoke rose from the bowl in an enigmatic curl, like a lock of hair. Steve took one of the cakes out of the box and carefully peeled away its silver case, which was pleated like an old lady's skirt. Matthews opened a door in the stove and prodded the glowing coals with a brass-handled poker.

'The milkman does eggs and bread and potatoes and butter and cheese,' he went on, 'but everything else I've had to do without. My legs are not what they were, you see. Fifty pence a week and tea thrown in, with a cake or some biscuits, whatever's going. What do you say?'

Steve gulped down the rest of his tea and picked the crumbs of the cake off the table with a moistened forefinger.

'I got to be going,' he said, standing up.

The way back along the basement passage, up the stairs and along the corridor seemed much shorter. Almost too soon, Steve found himself back in the chilly hallway. Before opening the front door, Matthews knelt down, lifted the flap of the letter-box and looked out for a long time.

'Can't be too careful,' he remarked. 'Times being what they are.'

Outside it was really cold. Steve told the old man he'd see him the following week and then ran off quickly. His thoughts, as he walked back to Trencham Road, were about money. The change which he had been told to keep the previous week had come to only a few pence in the end, and Steve had spent it on sweets, which he'd eaten on the way home. But if the old man was going to give him fifty pence every week that posed a problem. There was nowhere he could hide the money that the stotters might not look, nothing he could spend it on that they would not see. He didn't even want to think about what they might do if they found out that he'd been cheating them. The fate of his predecessors on the delivery round had been widely reported in the local media. One of the pensioners had sustained a dislocated hip, the other several fractured ribs. Dave admitted that once he got going he found it hard to stop. So the only course open to Steve really was to hand over the extra money, but it was going to be hard to explain this unexpected 25 per cent increase in the money he got for doing the paper round. He was still trying to think up a suitable story when he came to the main road he had to cross to get home. The traffic was heavy, as usual at this hour. It was while he was standing there, looking for an opening and worrying about what he was going to tell the stotters, that the grinning man appeared for the second time, bearing down on Steve like a demented soldier marching to destruction.

'Hey!' he called, his expression mocking and exultant. 'Hey, do you know what *time* it is?'

As he spoke, the vicious pent-up laughter that glittered in his eyes and twisted the muscles of his sweating face to breaking-point burst out, mutilating the words almost beyond recognition. He stood there, jerking and twitching all over, staring at the boy with such intensity it seemed he might be about to explode. Steve shook his head. The man's face screwed itself into a fierce grimace of contemptuous hostility, as if the boy was only pretending not to know, just to spite him. The sarcastic grin became bitterer than ever. 'What's the point in keeping up this pathetic farce?' it seemed to say. 'You don't think you fool *me*, do you?' A gap opened in the traffic and Steve took off, just beating a van that appeared out of nowhere. By the time he reached the other side and looked back, the man had gone.

Jimmy, Dave, Alex and Tracy were watching TV, the floor around them littered with cans of lager and take-out trays of chips with curry sauce. While he was wondering how they'd been able to pay for these luxuries, Steve realized that he hadn't come up with a story to explain the extra money. To his surprise however, Jimmy – usually stingily suspicious where money was concerned – didn't even bother to count the coins Steve gave him.

'What's this?' he jeered. 'You rob someone?'

For some reason this comment made Dave laugh, which effectively put an end to everything else for a while. Dave was not easily amused, but on the occasions when he did indulge he went all the way, whooping and yelping and howling, clutching his gut, drumming his heels on the floor and banging his forehead against the wall. But they were all in form that night, the stotters, for although the old woman Jimmy had selected as their target had been carrying less than he'd hoped, the hit itself had been a complete success and the take was still enough to pay for this modest celebration. The idea of using Tracy as bait had been fucking brill, if Jimmy did say so himself. People were always more trustful of girls, whatever they looked like. With attention focused on her, Dave was able to move in and get to work without any bother, while Alex and Jimmy kept look-out. No sweat! Jimmy couldn't see any reason why they shouldn't regularly supplement their income in the same way. Sooner or later they were bound to pick on someone who was carrying serious money, like that first time or even better. Then Jimmy would be off so fast these wankers wouldn't see him for dust. In keeping with the stotters' general policy towards the boy, Steve was kept out of this. All he knew was that everyone was in a good mood, that everything seemed to be going right. When Tracy passed out with one leg resting against his, warming him with a gentle radiance that penetrated his damp jeans like sunlight, the boy's happiness was complete.

The tasks which Ernest Matthews asked Steve to do for him became increasingly various as the weeks went by. As well as the supermarket, Steve visited the chemist, the newsagent, the stationer, the ironmonger, and the tobacconist's, where he passed as eighteen without any problem. He also went into the library and applied for a reader's ticket in order to keep the old man supplied with books.

'What do you want to read all these for?' Steve asked with a touch of resentment one day, after carrying back a particularly bulky load.

'They're all about the war,' Ernest Matthews replied. 'Written by famous historians.'

Steve wondered what a storian was. Someone who told stories, presumably.

The ultimate accolade came when he was sent to the post office to cash a countersigned pension cheque. By then almost a month had passed, and Steve had become thoroughly at home in the house in Grafton Avenue, where Ernest Matthews lived all alone in one room in the basement. He had even been taught a special way of ringing the doorbell so that the old man would know it was him. He wasn't quite sure why this was so important, and the question interested him the more in that he suspected that the answer might also explain why Matthews refused ever to venture outside the house itself. The old man's attempts to account for this no longer satisfied Steve.

'It's my legs, you see. They're not what they were. I find it hard to get about these days. Still, that's the way it goes, isn't it? Have you ever thought what it would be like if it went the *other* way, eh? If we were all born like I am now and then grew younger and healthier every day? And not just us, but everything around us too. Just imagine that! If every day a block of buildings disappeared and there was a green field there in its place. If there were fewer people around with every year that passed, so you'd get to know them better, of course, and every new face would be a great event. If the roads gradually shrank down to lanes where children could play the day away, and we all knew that tomorrow would be better still, and we'd be fresher and keener yet to enjoy it. Eh? Just imagine that!'

Steve nodded, although he couldn't see the attraction himself. He knew that his problems would all be solved once he ceased to be a child. But in any case, that was beside the point, a deliberate attempt by Matthews to distract attention from his initial statement. Steve wasn't fooled by the old man's claims about the state of his legs. He moved about the house with no sign of awkwardness or discomfort whatsoever. Steve didn't point this out, however, or demand to know the truth of the matter. In the end it emerged of its own accord one day as the boy was leaving.

'You haven't ever noticed anybody hanging about outside, I suppose?' Matthews asked before opening the front door. His tone was casual, but the intensity of his eyes gave him away. 'Anybody watching the house, following you when you leave, that sort of thing?'

Steve immediately thought of the grinning man, although he hadn't really been watching the house or following him. Ernest Matthews had noticed the boy's hesitation.

'You *have*?'

Steve nodded.

'When? Where?'

'The first time. And after that, when I was going back.'

Something had happened deep inside the old man's eyes, as if a blind had been drawn down.

'What did he look like?'

The boy considered for a moment.

'He walks funny, like he wants to pee. He smiles all the time too, only it's not really a smile.'

The old man was trembling with agitation.

'And he was watching this house, you say?'

In the end Steve nodded again. It was too late to correct himself now. He would have to stick to the story he'd told. It might well be true, anyway. The old man seemed to have been expecting something of the sort.

'Do you know him, then?' the boy asked.

The old man sighed deeply.

'Oh yes, I know him all right. It's a long story, lad. A long sad story. But I suppose you must hear it. It wouldn't be fair otherwise, asking you to come here and help me. It wouldn't be right, not if – '

He broke off, looking deeply troubled.

'But how *can* it be right? What if your mum and dad found out? What would they think of me?'

'That's all right,' Steve assured him. 'The people I live with, they don't care what happens to me.'

His only fear was that the old man might tell him to stop coming to the house every week. Matthews looked at him for a moment, as though considering what to do.

'I'll have to tell you the whole story,' he said finally, nodding to himself. 'Once you've heard it, you can decide whether you want to carry on coming or not.'

'I do!' the boy cried.

'You can't say that now. Not till you know what happened and who he is, that man you've seen. For now, just keep out of his way, if you can!'

He unbolted the front door and opened it cautiously.

'Keep out of his way!' he repeated as Steve scampered down the steps.

It was a clear freezing night. The sky seemed to be full of eyes.

FIVE

The Adolescent Unit in which Aileen Macklin worked formed part of a psychiatric hospital in North Kensington, overlooking the canal. The Unit itself occupied a separate block, with its own entrance and car-park, in the grounds of the main hospital, from which it was separated by a row of tall evergreens. The two buildings thus appeared to turn their backs on each other. Physically, too, they could hardly have been more different. The hospital was one of those redbrick monstrosities beloved by the Victorians and used by them virtually interchangeably as prisons, factories, hospitals, schools and barracks. It was lugubrious, authoritarian and massively institutional. It was also warm, dry, indestructible and as functionally effective as the day it was built. The Adolescent Unit, thoughtfully screened from this vision of the past by the conifers, had been run up in the early sixties, seemingly with a view to reversing all the qualities of its Victorian parent. In this it had proved remarkably successful. Although its originally spacious rooms had been subdivided and partitioned under pressure for space, the building remained determinedly casual and easy-going. It was also damp, draughty, cold and slowly falling to bits. Aileen found its air of faded, tatty idealism as depressing as the broken-spined, brittle-paged paperbacks by Laing ('Brighton, 4/10/68') or Leary ('Ya blow my mind – and other things! Ray'), which she occasionally came across on her shelves while looking for something else.

Her office was not in the Unit itself, which had proved to be hopelessly inadequate to the demands made on it as the years went by. As facilities elsewhere in the city closed down, patients who were too ill to be discharged were concentrated in those that remained open. Since there had also been a marked rise in the incidence of psychiatric disorder, particularly among young people, this resulted in the Unit throwing out annexes, wings and extensions whose construction methods and materials grew progressively cruder as budgets fell. Aileen's office occupied half of a prefabricated hut supported on brick stilts that had originally been knocked up as a temporary storage space a decade or so earlier and then retained because it was there. It had a flat tarred roof which leaked, flooring that sagged underfoot, windows which contrived to rattle no matter how many cardboard wedges were jammed into them and doors you had to kick open yet admitted every draught going. It was sweltering in summer, freezing in winter, and stank obscurely all year round. Jenny Wilcox, the occupational therapist who shared the hut with Aileen, had once remarked that it was enough to drive anyone mad.

Aileen could usually tell what sort of day she was going to have by the way she felt as she turned into the driveway separating the Adolescent Unit from the main road. Sometimes it seemed like a horizontal level in a mine: a deep, dark, narrow tunnel leading to a place of relentless unrewarding labour. At other times the same stretch of tarmac reminded her of an old advertisement for a brand of children's shoes, showing a straight open highway leading to worthy achievements and a brighter future. That Wednesday, the day after she had visited Gary Dunn at the Assessment Centre, the driveway seemed quite simply to offer refuge.

It had been a bad night. Douglas had had it all his way at the dinner table the evening before, although Aileen knew that she could and should have denied him. He had used one of his oldest and simplest ploys, piling up references to his own prestige and success until she was drawn into trying to retaliate. That was fatal, of course, for whatever she might think of him – and whatever he might think of himself, in his heart of hearts, where Aileen knew that he nourished the most tormenting doubts – there was no question that as far as the world was concerned, Douglas Macklin was a high-flyer. Wasn't he off to America at the end of that very week for yet another top-level international conference? So when Aileen presumed to mention her own career it was easy for him – a smile, a glance, a raised eyebrow was enough – to make her look not only intellectually second-rate but vulgarly me-tooish into the bargain, insisting on equal time for her lacklustre accomplishments. As if that hadn't been enough, Aileen seemed to be beginning one of the cycles of insomnia from which she had suffered since childhood, and in the intermittent patches of sleep which she had been able to snatch as she lay listening to Douglas's ripe complacent snores, she had once again had the 'flying' dream.

As usual, she had no memory of the dream itself, but she knew what had happened the moment she awakened by the way she felt: blissfully relaxed and calm, as though something of the still pale glow that pervaded the dream had remained with her, casting a gentle luminance on all her thoughts. Then she had suddenly broken out in a cold sweat as she remembered the terrible significance this dream had acquired since Raymond's death, how she had nearly died too, only surviving by a miracle which had cost the life of her unborn child. This was what always happened now, the beauty followed by the horror. The dream had lost its innocence. Deliberately, she had forced herself to get out of bed, go downstairs, make a cup of tea and listen to drivel on the radio until exhaustion calmed her.

It was thus with positive relief that she brought the red Mini to rest in the slot marked DR REITH, commemorating her predecessor who had died more than ten years earlier. She picked up Gary Dunn's file, which she had taken home to study, and walked to her office with a feeling of anticipation. The day before her was filled with things to do, tasks to perform, duties to carry out and problems to resolve. Perhaps none of it was very glorious or noteworthy by her husband's standards, but it was work that had to be done just the same. And doing it would be a sweet relief from the mental jumble she felt growing in volume all the time, as if all the junk she had accumulated in the attic over the years had started to breed and multiply, spilling out of its confinement, pushing down to invade the rest of the house.

When Aileen appeared in the doorway between their two offices, Jenny Wilcox was sipping a mug of Nescafé and throwing darts at a board printed with Mrs Thatcher's features.

'Fancy a game?' she asked. 'You get one for the hair, five for the chin, ten for the nose, twenty for the good eye and fifty for the wonky one. An arrow in the heart wins you the game.'

Aileen inspected the board more closely.

'The point being . . .' she began.

'That there isn't one. Exactly.'

Jenny beamed gleefully back at Aileen. The occupational therapist was a short, dark woman with an intensity and directness of manner usually associated with Latin blood, but which in Jenny's case was an ideological choice: this was how she felt that women should relate to each other. A snub nose and straight black hair cut in the shape of a helmet gave her a rather engaging tomboy look, and when she smiled, as she did often, her upper lip rose to reveal a startling expanse of pink gum. But there was nothing childish about Jenny. She was bright, breezy, upbeat, combative and totally dedicated to her patients. Aileen considered her a good therapist, an excellent union rep and an invigorating and supportive colleague, but not quite a friend. There were various reasons for this, of which the most obvious was Jenny's husband, a researcher for London Weekend Television whose one ambition in life was to get 'front of camera'. Jon's interest in other people depended entirely on whether he thought they might help him to achieve this. Aileen's problem was not avoiding him – Jon wasted no time on those he couldn't use – but coming to terms with the fact that Jenny had married him. That cast a shadow on her which Aileen could never quite forget. If Jenny was as nice as she seemed, how could she stand living with such a creep? Was her warmth to Aileen just a façade, a bit of feminist window-dressing? Or – and this was the really unpleasant thought – did she have Jon to thank for it? Did the Wilcoxes have an unspoken demarcation agreement whereby Jenny looked after being positive and jolly while Jon handled selfishness and insensitivity? Aileen was only too aware that couples didn't stay together by chance. However ill-suited or unhappy they might appear, if the relationship lasted it was because it worked, although the exact nature of the work might well remain obscure to the couple themselves, perhaps necessarily so.

'Do you remember a boy called Gary Dunn?' she asked as

Jenny sent her final dart winging across the room to embed itself in the Prime Minister's ear.

The therapist pursed her lips for a moment, staring up at the warped insulation tiles on the ceiling of the hut.

'Hang about. Wasn't he the one with aural hallucinations of a schizophrenic kind and a taste for over-the-top mad scenes?'

'He's moved up to arson attempts now. Equally unconvincing, I'm glad to say. Anyway, he's coming in for a few days and I'd like to try to make sure he settles down without too much difficulty. I seem to remember he used to like craftwork. Would it be all right to send him along as soon as he arrives this morning?'

'Of course. The workshop's just the place for an aspiring fire-raiser. Shall I leave some paraffin out or will he be bringing his own?'

Aileen was used to Jenny's manner and made no reply beyond a smile. She made no attempt to explain her real reason for wanting Gary sent to the workshop immediately he arrived at the Unit. It was as if everything connected with the boy had been contaminated by the secret that Aileen concealed even from herself as far as possible: her irrational identification of Gary Dunn with the child she had conceived with Raymond. That simply wasn't a matter she could mention, even to Jenny, and this prohibition created others, until Aileen found herself acting in a devious manner that was quite foreign to her.

After discussing the matter with the consultant the day before, Aileen had been able to phone Pamela Haynes and tell her that Gary would be admitted to the Unit for a period of 'observation'. The social worker was due to bring him in between nine and ten o'clock that morning. Aileen was tied up with a therapy group until half past ten, but as soon as that was over she made her way to the ward where Gary had been allocated a bed which was unoccupied for a few days pending the arrival of a patient from another hospital. She hurried through the sitting room, painted in the deep pastel green from which the ward took its name, and quickly located the boy's bed. On the counterpane lay a blue canvas bag containing Gary Dunn's few worldly goods. Aileen sorted through them like a customs officer. She found what she was looking for almost immediately.

She did not speak to the boy until after lunch, when he was brought to the sitting room in Yellow Ward to take part in a group therapy session. She thought that she had prepared herself adequately for this further encounter, visualizing the moment again and again until its power wore out, but the moment the boy entered the room she felt as though she were standing at the edge of an abyss with him at the other side, calling out to her in a silent scream, like the whistles only dogs can hear. No preparation or visualization, nothing she could do, had any power against that naked reality. This time the resemblance to Raymond seemed, for the moment or two that the sensation lasted, so strong that Aileen was tempted for the first time to wonder if it might not be real. But she immediately dismissed the idea with horror. That way, she knew, lay madness.

Yellow Ward was on the second floor of the Unit. The outer wall, like all those in the building, consisted of a pattern of rectangular panels, half of them panes of glass and the rest opaque. This chessboard design covered the length of both sides of the Unit without concessions to the size or shape of the rooms inside. In the sitting room there was one sliver of window at floor level and a patch of another crouching in one corner of the ceiling, together with a whole pane set just too high to show anything but the tips of the trees lining the drive. The bright yellow paint gave the light in the room a slightly hysterical quality, accentuating the marks on the boy's face from the beating the other boys at the hostel had given him. But there was a new calmness in his eyes and manner as he took his place in one of the vinyl-covered chairs, and it saddened Aileen to think of what she was going to have to do. But there was no help for it. The boy couldn't stay, and that was all there was to it.

As on his earlier visits to the Unit, Gary took no part in the discussion, although he listened attentively and tried not to look bored. But Aileen was no longer concerned with involving him in the dynamics of the group. The ordinary rules and methods did not apply in this case. She made no attempt to speak to him until the session was over and they were alone.

'Well, so here you are,' she began brightly, sitting down in the chair next to him, its spongy seat still warm and sculpted from the previous posterior. 'Do you still think it was worth all that effort to get in here?'

The boy frowned and said nothing.

'What about those voices you were telling me about yesterday?' Aileen continued. 'The ones you said told you to set fire to the curtains and not to trust the doctors, not to take your pills and so on. Has anything else like that happened?'

Gary stared at the floor for a while, as though trying to remember.

'That nurse who brought me here, she was talking to all the people we passed, telling them about me, all the bad things I've done. And they agreed. They all said I should kill myself.'

Aileen looked at him in silence.

'If we're to help you, Gary,' she said at last, 'you must tell us the truth.'

The boy looked up at her for the first time.

'I *have*!'

His tone was obstinate, resentful. His eyes held hers with stubborn persistence. Aileen opened her suede shoulder-bag and took out a book wrapped in a dirty sheet of brown paper torn roughly at the edges. She removed it, revealing a bright glossy cover with the title *Schizophrenia: What It Is And What It Isn't*. On the fly-leaf there was a gummed sheet printed 'Hammersmith Public Libraries' with a list of rubber-stamped dates, the last being several months earlier, in the middle of July. Aileen consulted the index and flicked through the pages to a chapter headed 'Symptoms'.

' "Aural hallucinations",' she read aloud. ' "One of the commonest symptoms of schizophrenia. Patients may complain of hearing voices telling them to kill themselves, or not to take their medication, or not to trust their doctor. At other times their family or strangers may be heard discussing them in a cold and threatening way." '

'You're not going to send me away again, are you?' the boy broke out.

His voice was trembling, his eyes a wild glitter.

'That depends on you. This is not a hostel, you know. It's a hospital. People come here to get better, and we can't help you get better if you go on pretending. Do you understand?'

The boy nodded without looking at her.

'Why did you borrow this book?' Aileen asked casually.

'She wrote it down, that word.'

He pointed to the title of the book.

'Who did?'

'Pam.'

'Pamela Haynes? Your social worker?'

The boy nodded grudgingly.

'You saw her write the word "schizophrenia"?'

'She went outside to talk to someone.'

'And you looked at her notepad while she was gone?'

'You won't send me away, will you?' he pleaded. 'He'll kill me if you do!'

'Who'll kill you?'

'The man I told you about! Hazchem.'

'What did you say?'

But the boy's moment of desperation had passed, and he would not repeat the word or phrase – was it 'Ask him'? – which Aileen had failed to catch, merely shaking his head and rocking from side to side, hugging himself tightly.

On the way back to her office, Aileen ran into the consultant psychiatrist's assistant, a tubby balding man whose attempts to look like a smooth City gent were defeated by a prominent bottom which stuck out like a belly turned the wrong way round. Aileen described the outcome of her interview with Gary Dunn.

'It's been the social worker's fault all along. She got so excited about having made a diagnosis of schizophrenia all by her big self that she left her notes lying around where the boy could see them.'

'Very unprofessional,' the assistant agreed. 'Still, you've got to hand it to the little bugger, haven't you? Top marks for initiative and all that. But what's his game? Why he's so keen to be admitted to the Unit that he spends his spare time swotting up symptoms with a copy of *Teach Yourself Schizophrenia*?'

'I don't know. He claims someone's trying to kill him. For some reason he seems to think he's safe here.'

The assistant fingered his pudgy jowls.

'As long as he doesn't eat the food. Still, we can't keep a bed tied up just to keep him happy. Out-patient care, of course, all he wants. But beds are just too precious.'

He was right, of course, and Aileen knew it. Even with its various annexes and extensions, the Unit was designed to house no more than eighty resident patients. By dint of placing beds in corridors and service areas this number had been increased to ninety-five. Over two hundred other patients on a waiting list were currently being housed in regional general hospitals, where they received little or no psychiatric care, with the result that their condition progressively deteriorated.

'It's only until Friday,' Aileen stressed. 'There's a bed that's free anyway.'

'That's the day after tomorrow!' the assistant reminded her. 'What do you expect to achieve in that space of time?'

'Nothing, probably. But at least it'll stop the local authority turning him over to the police for the arson attempt.'

'And afterwards where will he go?'

'I don't know!' she retorted crossly, feeling browbeaten. 'I don't know anything.'

But when she got home that evening, Aileen knew one more thing at least. She had stopped at the public library on the way and returned the book on schizophrenia, paying the fine herself. The librarian proceeded to give her a brisk lecture about withholding books needed by other readers, and to justify herself Aileen started to explain about Gary Dunn.

'What has this Gary Dunn got to do with it?' the librarian interrupted peevishly.

'He's the boy who borrowed the book.'

'Not according to my records.'

The librarian's tone suggested that if there was a discrepancy between reality and his records, then reality was most probably at fault. To clinch the matter, he showed Aileen the computer entry. *Schizophrenia: What It Is And What It Isn't* had been borrowed on 6 July by Steven Bradley, of 2 Grafton Avenue. His ticket had been issued in February of the same year, the application being endorsed by Ernest Matthews Esq., a ratepayer at the same address.

SIX

'It all happened very long ago and very far away. Whenever I think of that time I remember a trip we took once, to the seaside. It was the only time I was ever away from home, you see, and the first time I'd been on a train, so it stuck in my mind. I remember the doors were inches thick, as heavy as a gate. My mother warned me, "You catch your fingers in that and it'll have them off as quick as trimming carrots." My mother didn't like trains. She said you got fleas off the seats. I don't suppose mothers have changed much, have they? Anyway, *I* must have liked it, because here I am, near eighty years on and I can see it as well as I can see you, my lad. To open the window you had to pull down on a thick leather strap, like at the barber's, only it had holes punched in it to take a brass peg. You let the strap run back inside the door, the window came rattling down and you could look out. There was a smell of smoke and a spray of wet steam in the air, and every once in a while you'd get a smut of soot in your eye that set you blinking. That's what I remember most from that holiday, that and the pier where we went in the afternoon to listen to the band. There was a flight of metal steps, just like a staircase, which went down into the water at the end of the pier. As the waves passed, in the troughs between them, you could see that the steps went on down below the water, all covered in barnacles and seaweed, but still as solid as ever. If I close my eyes I can still see that staircase leading down into the sea and hear the band playing and see the clouds drifting across the sky, as big and calm as battleships . . .'

They were sitting in the snug clutter of the basement room in Grafton Avenue, the old man and the boy. To celebrate the commencement of the story he had promised to tell, Ernest Matthews had prepared a high tea of soft-boiled eggs with bread and butter cut into inch-wide fingers. Steve had been instructed at some length in the correct method of opening his egg, by tapping the shell repeatedly with his spoon and then peeling off the shards and the silky clinging inner membrane. When they finished eating, the old man had retired to his armchair and lit the pipe that now lay forgotten in his hand. Steve sat by the table, his eyes fixed on the stove, where rising currents of hot air made the tiles of the fireplace ripple like stones on the bed of a stream.

'I remember the sea, too,' the old man went on. 'It seemed so big, so endless, and all in movement. I'd only seen the countryside before, and round our way that was all tucks and folds, so you couldn't see far. Later on, I found out that once upon a time all that land had been under water too, and that the hills I used to walk upon were made of the skeletons of the creatures that lived in those ancient seas. Just imagine, those hills and valleys, the very houses, were all made of nothing but dead bodies! I lived in a cemetery, lad, and thought it a paradise.'

He put his pipe between his lips and torched it briefly with the lighter.

'But we must get on, and keep to the story, or we'll never have done. The trouble is, this skull of mine is packed with memories like the inside of a golf ball, and once I get started there's no stopping me. First I must tell you about the Hall. Now take this house here. What we're in now is the kitchen, as was. There's two more rooms like it downstairs, as well as any amount of cupboards and larders and so on. On the first floor there's the sitting room and dining room, and three bedrooms above that, making eight rooms in all, not counting the attic. There are many meaner houses than this, I dare say, and yet to call it by the same name as the one where I grew up seems a sort of insult to the language. I'm not speaking about the architecture, mind, though I dare say that there was plenty of that too. It was Elizabethan, you see, which is why the shape of it was like a capital E, with two wings at either end and the great hall jutting out in the centre. But all that meant nothing to me, though I liked the idea, Elizabeth being my mother's name. What I never got over was how big it all was. Why, this place would have fitted into it twenty or thirty times over! When I was very young, I thought the Hall was a kind of plant that put out new growth each year, for there always seemed to be rooms I hadn't seen before, doors I hadn't opened. It wasn't till I was ten or eleven that I began to understand how it all fitted together, and even by the end it was still full of surprises.'

'Was your mother a princess?' Steve asked.

The boy spoke so rarely, and only then in response to a question, that the old man glanced at him with surprise. Then he laughed out loud.

'Good Lord above, you don't think it was *our* house, do you?' He pointed to the electric light above their heads. 'You see that? And the stove here? And the water pipes? *That's* what we were, my lad, nothing more nor less. For there was no light then, once the sun went down, but what you made yourself. That meant fifteen or twenty oil lamps to be cleaned and filled and brought to every room, scenting the whole place with their sweet, warm smell. As for the water, that had to be fetched from the spring, and if you wanted tea or a bath it had to be warmed on the stove. Wood had to be cut and hauled and stacked and laid for the fires, which had to be cleaned out early each morning and then relit. All of that made work for idle hands to do, believe you me. Cooks and housemaids and kitchen maids and still-room maids and laundry maids and I don't know what else besides, with a housekeeper to make sure they did it properly. And that was my mother.'

He broke off again to get his pipe going, sucking the flame down into the bowl in a way that fascinated Steve, who imagined the flame continuing through the pipe and down the old man's throat, blazing in his stomach like the stove.

'But you're right, too, in a way,' Matthews went on. 'The Hall *was* ours, for unlike these wires and tubes and pipes that do the necessary nowadays, we were alive and we lived there. There were rules, of course. Doors we weren't allowed to open, rooms that were out of bounds. But that only counted when the family were there, which was only a few months in the summer. So in a way it was our house even more than it was theirs. Mine above all, perhaps, for as a child I was treated with indulgence, and my mother being the housekeeper was above all the staff except the butler. My father, I should explain, had been one of the gardeners until he fell out of a tree and broke his neck. I don't really remember him.'

The muffled muggy silence of the room reformed for a few moments.

'What about *your* parents?' Matthews asked, looking round at Steve. 'Don't you live with them?'

The boy jerked his head aside. It was a warning, but the old man paid no heed.

'Ran away, did you?'

Steve twisted his head to the other side in a convulsive movement which might have been taken for a negation.

'Or are they . . .?' the old man began tentatively. But Steve was on his feet and shouting.

'What you asking me all this for? This ain't got fuck to do with it! You're supposed to be telling me about what happened, about that man, not asking me a lot of shit like you was the police or something!'

The old man seemed to wilt visibly under the boy's furious gaze. His hands dithered aimlessly about in his lap.

'I'm sorry, lad. Sorry. I won't ask again, I promise.'

He turned away and poked the fire, clearing his throat apologetically. After a while Steve sat down again.

'You said we got to stick to the story,' he muttered.

'Quite right, quite right.'

'Well, you better,' the boy warned. 'Because I seen him again, that man. When I got here tonight. He was standing right outside, staring at the house like it was made of glass and he could see everything you do!'

Steve considered this a fair return for the pain the old man had given him. Tit for tat was the rule the world ran on, he knew that much. You had to do your bit to keep things in balance or there was no saying what might happen. Besides, it was only relatively untrue, for he *had* seen the grinning man again, though not that evening and not outside Matthews's house. It had happened earlier in the week, when Steve was on his way back from collecting the stotters' social security cheques from the letter-box in the council block they used as a convenience address. This was in White City, a fair old step from the newspaper round, so it had been all the more startling to find the grinning man there, striding along the pavement on the other side of the road. There was no mistaking that frenetic motion, though, like someone having an epileptic fit on his feet. He didn't appear to have noticed the boy, so Steve decided to follow him and see where he was going. Ernest Matthews had made it clear that he was terrified of this man, and he would therefore presumably welcome any information Steve could provide about him. Keeping a safe distance, and dodging into doorways or behind parked cars whenever necessary, Steve followed the grinning man all the way up Wood Lane. Just before the canal the man turned right and continued for another half-mile or so before disappearing into an imposing gateway. Steve approached with great caution, fearing that it might be a trap. Inside the gates, at the end of a short drive, was a large brick building which looked like a prison. The man was nowhere to be seen. Attached to a wire fence at the side of the building was an orange sign with black lettering which read 'WARNING HAZCHEM'.

'Outside the house!' Matthews echoed. 'Staring at it! This is new. This is not good.'

His hands rubbed together as if trying to comfort each other. Too late, Steve realized that he would not now be able to tell the old man what he had found out. That was the problem with telling stories. It seemed all right at the time, but then they got out of control. Still, it wasn't important. For now he was content to relish this new sense of power. All his short life, Steve had been the one to be terrified by others. To find himself creating fear rather than suffering it was a delicious sensation, and completely justified by the principle of tit for tat. Steve still had a long, long way to go before he had repaid all the fear which he had been made to feel! And it was all right, because his story had been untrue. If Hazchem, as Steve now thought of him, had really been watching the house and he hadn't told Matthews, that might have been serious. But how could something that had never happened do anyone any harm?

'Ah, lad, I should never have involved you in this terrible business,' the old man sighed, shaking his head once more. 'I should never have invited you into the house that day. It was wrong of me, very wrong. But it can't be helped now. You *are* in, and he knows you are, so the only thing to do is get on as quickly as we can, so that at least you know the danger. Now next I must tell you something about the family. They weren't county, like you might suppose, but in trade. Jeffries' Biscuits used to be a household name at the time, though you won't find them nowadays. They came in square metal tins with a paper label with the name spelt out in big black capitals with edges and shading and a picture of a boy sitting on a hill looking at a sunset, all in royal blue and red. Maurice and Rupert, the two sons, used the empty boxes as forts, up in the playroom. They had toy artillery pieces that fired little pins, and clockwork trains that ran all round the room, under the legs of the furniture and through tin tunnels painted with shrubs and grass. They had warships too, made of lead, and others they made themselves, cut out of cardboard and glued together and painted grey. I used to go up there when the family was away. Many an afternoon I spent wandering through those rooms full of furniture draped in huge dust-sheets, like an Army camp. Sometimes I'd get lost and catch a beating for being late to tea, for everyone had to be punctual in those days, gentry and staff alike. There were no exceptions.

'Now all this makes Maurice and Rupert Jeffries sound like children, but in fact by the time I'm talking of they were almost twenty and both at university. Their mother had passed away some years earlier and there were no other children, so when old man Jeffries died, the same year as the king it was, the staff at the Hall were anxious they'd all be dismissed. I remember my mother discussing it with the butler and the cook. "This'll mean change!" they agreed. "The young masters won't want to keep this old place." You see country houses then were two a penny. No one wanted them, because the land didn't pay no more. And so it looked as though the Hall would be given up and we'd all be turned out to seek positions elsewhere. My mother and the other staff were resigned to this prospect, for they knew how the world wagged. But I'd spent my whole life at the Hall and in the village and countryside round about. I couldn't believe that all that could be taken away from me by the whim of two young striplings barely older than I was myself. My mother tried to explain, but to me it sounded as crazy as hearing that the river which ran down our valley would stop flowing because someone had signed a bit of paper to that effect. Nevertheless, that was the position, and turned out we would no doubt have been if it hadn't been for cunning old Jeffries.

'Maurice's and Rupert's father had left a will stipulating that his estate was to be divided equally between the two sons, but that no part of it was to be sold, let or otherwise alienated or disposed of without the signature of both. No great stumbling block there, you might think. Twin brothers, brought up together from the cradle, should have been able to agree on what to do. Ah, but that was it, you see! They couldn't. Never had been able to, never would be able to. If Maurice wanted one thing, then as sure as night follows day Rupert would set his heart on the opposite. No one knew the reason why, only that it was so. I once heard the butler say that if one of them asked for port wine he knew to offer the other madeira. It was the same when they went to university. No sooner had Maurice announced that he was going to Cambridge than his brother promptly settled on Oxford. Which was all to the good, as it turned out, for that was not so far away, and Rupert was able to spend much of his time at the Hall. He was our favourite, by a long way. He relished all the country had to offer, the hunting and shooting and fishing, and he took an interest in everyone who lived and worked on the estate. He knew all the villagers by name and would stop and inquire after their health. He used to organize a big tea for them once a year, too, which was considered a great treat in those days. Maurice, on the other hand, was a townee through and through. Even when he did venture down to the Hall, days would pass without him setting foot outside the front door. It was all books and pictures and conversation with him. His favourite exercise was lying on the sofa smoking a cigarette and passing remarks in foreign languages with his clever friends. But he spent most of his time in London, or running around on the Continent. Which suited us just fine, because when he did take it into his head to come down with a party of guests then all hell broke loose. Breakfast at eight, that was a meal in itself, six or more courses. Lunch at half past one, about eight or ten courses there. Tea in the afternoon, then dinner at eight thirty, with twelve courses. Then there were the rooms to be cleaned and heated, for these folk weren't like Rupert, who slept with the window open all year round and could never abide a fire. There were baths to draw, linen to air and iron, provisions to order, and if everything wasn't just right and dead on time someone would catch it. But luckily Maurice's visits were rare and didn't last long, for he and his sophisticated pals soon got bored with the simple pleasures of the country. As for Master Rupert, he was so easy to care for you'd hardly know he was there, as my mother used to say. His rooms were in the east wing of the Hall, where the guest rooms were, but he was the easiest guest you'd ever hope to entertain, for he was always out, walking or riding from dawn to dusk. As for his meals, he'd bring home a trout he'd hooked, and be content with that and a plain roast. He went out shooting or fishing every day, depending on the season.

'As I said, Maurice and Rupert didn't see eye to eye on anything, and whenever Maurice appeared at the hall we knew that sooner or later there would be ructions. Maurice was far too genteel ever to raise his voice, but he had a way of describing what his brother thought or did that made it sound ridiculous. For instance he might tell his guests, "Now if any of you are depraved enough to be up with the lark tomorrow morning, if you happen to glance out of your window, you may see a figure tripping stealthily across the lawn. Do not be alarmed. It is neither fawn nor satyr, but merely my brother Rupert, off to commune with Nature, that great dynamo whence he draws those mystic powers, which, as you have doubtless remarked, cause him to hum and crackle with energy and charm." We had all this from the butler, who waited at table and could do Maurice to a T. Rupert gave as good as he got, though, only there was none of this sly insinuating manner about him. He'd come right out and say what he thought. "This country is decaying like fine timber with dry rot. There's nothing to show on the surface as yet, but at the heart the old vigour and vibrancy is gone. And the fungi that have caused this, the canker that is consuming our great heritage, is composed of tiny crawling creatures like you and your friends, Maurice. Men who have sold their souls to progress and the mob, who go whoring after strange gods and neglect the spirits of their native land, who spice their corrupt and decadent conversation with foreign catchphrases yet have so far forgotten their own tongue that they call their cowardice pacifism, their ignorance science, their treachery socialism and their lack of virility civilization." Oh, he didn't mince his words, our Rupert, I can assure you! But Maurice and his friends didn't seem to mind. They just smiled in a superior way, as though Rupert were some sort of country show they'd come down on purpose to see.'

The old man broke off to relight his pipe.

'Are you following all this?' he asked.

Steve shrugged.

'Go on. I like hearing you talk.'

'Well, that's very convenient, because it happens to be the thing I like best myself. Anyway, according to the terms of old Jeffries' will, with the two brothers at loggerheads nothing could be changed, which suited us down to the ground. My mother and the rest of the staff all kept their places and I wasn't robbed of the only life I'd ever known, not yet. Then that last summer, just before the war, much to everyone's surprise Maurice suddenly came to live at the Hall. Naturally this caused problems, not just for Rupert, who expected to have the place pretty much to himself, but for the staff, who had grown rather too used to idleness. No one seemed able to explain Maurice's abrupt change of heart. By this time I had turned sixteen, and was helping out in the garden. They hoped I would take after my father, who they said could make a dead plant sprout again. At any rate, one day I was hoeing some beds when I heard somebody say, ". . . because I'm in love!". It was Mr Maurice's voice, coming from the alley just behind the hedge where I was working. I heard the crunch of footsteps on the gravel, and then another voice replied, "In love! Why, Maurice, I fall in love at least once a week, on average, but I shouldn't dream of deserting my friends and burying myself away in the depths of the country like some hermit." Naturally all this whetted my curiosity. The head gardener was nowhere about, so I set off along the service path, which ran parallel to the walk that the two gentlemen were on. The hedge between us was so high that although we were just a foot or two apart, they were no more aware of me than of the man in the moon. I missed the next few words, but I caught up with them in time to hear Maurice saying, " . . . the most ravishing female I have ever set eyes on." "But who was she?" the other man enquired. I'd recognized him by now. It was one of Maurice's closest friends, a young man named Aubrey Deville. "That's just it," Maurice went on, "I haven't the slightest idea."

'By now they had reached what we called the fountain, a rock pool with carp swimming in it. They sat down on the stone bench there and after swearing his friend to the strictest secrecy, Maurice told him the whole story. It had started about a month before, he said, when he came down to the Hall for one of his brief visits. "You may recall, Aubrey, that after dinner we went to the billiard room and stayed there until two or three in the morning. Well perhaps it was the excitement of watching my brother being made an ass of by young Sullivan, but at any rate I found that I simply could not get to sleep. At last I gave it up and sat down at my writing-desk to catch up on my correspondence. The desk stands directly before the window, and thus commands an excellent view of the lawn. Well, I had been sitting there for some time when my eye was suddenly drawn by a movement outside. My first thought was that it must be a fox or a badger, but I very soon saw that the figure was human. The house had been as still as a grave for several hours, and I knew that it could not be one of us. I feared it might be an intruder, perhaps a poacher or even a housebreaker.

' "The moon that night was just a day or two off the full, and the lawn gleamed brightly except where the shadows of the two great beeches fell, as dark and dense as clay. At first the figure was in the shadow of the easterly beech, a mere glimmer of whiteness in the night, but as I watched it moved out into the open. *It was a woman, Aubrey*! She was wearing a sort of white shift which left her arms and lower legs bare. Her hair was all let down, too, so that she looked as though she had just risen from her bed. She moved slowly and gracefully across the lawn, looking about her at the house and the gardens as though it was the most natural thing in the world. My brain was in an absolute turmoil, yet I could not move, could hardly even breathe! I simply sat there, transfixed, as she crossed the lawn and was swallowed up by the shadow of the other tree. No sooner had she vanished than I felt as though I had been released from a spell. I dressed hurriedly, rushed downstairs and ran out on to the lawn, but there was no one there. I searched the whole garden, which was illuminated as brightly as on a winter day, but I could find absolutely no trace of the woman. At last I returned to my room and watched the lawn until it grew light, but all in vain. And as I sat there, exhausted and hollow-eyed, I realized with dismay that I had fallen in love. Her frank bold freedom, her candour, her purity! She is the woman I've always dreamed of, the woman for whom I've been searching all my life! Ah, Aubrey, if only you'd seen her! But you *must* see her. You *shall* see her!" '

The old man broke off as the chimes of the squat walnut-cased clock on the mantelpiece struck six.

'I like that sound,' Steve murmured.

'You should have heard the clock that stood in the housekeeper's parlour at the Hall,' the old man told him. 'Its chimes were as mellow as the drops of wine I used to taste out of the gentlemen's glasses sometimes after dinner. And all day long and all through the night the pendulum swung to and fro, tick, tock, tick, tock. Ah, things were different then! There were sixty minutes to the hour in those days. Now the time is nothing but rubbish, short measure and shoddy quality. Still, we must try and make better use of it next week, or we'll never be done.'

Steve walked home that evening with a faint smile on his lips. Naturally he didn't believe a word of what the old man had told him. Countryside under the sea! Houses that grew like plants! People who kept snacking all day but were so poor they didn't even have electricity like the stotters! Matthews couldn't even get his story straight. He'd talked about a big house, but before that he'd said he used to live in a cemetery. Steve had slept in a cemetery once, up Stoke Newington way. It hadn't been too bad, until a gang of Irish gypsy kids shut him up in one of those little houses they had for the dead people. As for old Matthews, Steve was beginning to suspect that he was a bit round the twist. What he'd said about his skull being like a golf ball, *that* made sense all right! Steve had found a golf ball in a park once. It had been cracked along one side, and when he'd prised it open he'd found a crazy mess of tiny rubber threads inside, all squashed together higgledy-piggledy. That was what the old man's skull must be like inside all right, a right mess. But Steve wouldn't let on to the old man that he'd sussed him out. He had too much to lose. There was the warmth, the food, the tea, the money, the weekly appointments that gave him a future to look forward to. Above all, there was the old man's fear. Steve loved to feel it, to bask in it. It enveloped him like a fur coat, a luxury he had never been able to afford before and which might be taken from him at any moment.

SEVEN

Aileen had until Friday to find out why the boy she still thought of as Gary Dunn wanted so desperately to be confined in a psychiatric hospital. By the time she left work on Thursday afternoon, it had become clear that he wasn't going to help her. She had played her big card that morning, telling the boy about her visit to the library, and her discovery that the book about schizophrenia which she'd found among his belongings had been borrowed by someone called Steven Bradley. He had reacted as though she'd struck him, which only confirmed Aileen's conviction that this was not just another alias but his real name.

But nothing else had budged. She had probed and pushed, almost pleaded in the end, but all in vain. He had simply shrugged off her questions in his usual sulky, uncommunicative manner. By the end of their conversation, Aileen was beginning to feel that panicky sense of suffocation which overcame her in the course of her dinner-table duels with Douglas. Gary's strategy and tactics were the opposite of her husband's – the weapons of the poor, the uneducated, the inarticulate – but the result was much the same. Douglas made her feel depressed about being stupid and unsuccessful, Gary made her feel guilty for being powerful and privileged. She had already given him what he wanted – admission to the Unit – and he evidently felt that he had nothing to gain by making any further concessions. On the contrary, if he got well again he'd have to leave. He therefore had every reason not to co-operate.

In every other respect the boy was proving to be a model patient. He behaved rather as though the Unit were an exclusive club to which he had been lucky enough to be elected. He neither sought nor avoided attention, taking his cue from the other patients but keeping his distance so as not to offend anyone. He had proved to be an instant success with the hard-pressed nursing staff: not only did he give them no trouble, but on several occasions a nurse dealing with one of the more problematic inmates would find that Gary had quietly but effectively sorted out a minor crisis among the other boys while her back was turned. In short, everything was wonderful, except that his name wasn't Gary and he wasn't eighteen years old or mentally ill. Aileen saw no hope of solving the riddle of his behaviour before he was expelled from his fool's paradise the following day. In a last desperate gesture she had phoned the police and passed on the boy's real name in hopes that their Missing Persons section might be able to trace his family. But nothing altered the fact that the next day the boy would be taken away from her and handed back to the local authority, his secret still locked away inside him like an unexploded bomb.

By five o'clock that afternoon Aileen felt that she had to talk to someone. Jenny Wilcox was the only conceivable possibility. It even occurred to Aileen that this might be an opportunity for them to get to know each other better, to become real friends. It was no doubt her own fault that it hadn't happened yet. She had always held back from the younger woman, maintaining a coolness and irony that were the classic hallmarks of defensiveness. As for the dreaded Jon, was Jenny, with all her virtues, to be discarded simply because Aileen didn't approve of her partner? The fact of the matter was that it had been *she*, Aileen, who had refused to be warm and open and intimate all along. Well, here was a perfect chance to set matters straight.

Aileen's route back to her office took her down a ground-floor corridor and out through a side door of the main building. The therapeutically uplifting colours of the wards had been abandoned here in favour of basic bureaucratic grey. Aileen had passed through the swing doors at the end of the corridor at least four times a day for over ten years, but she had never actually looked at them before. But now, as she raised her hand to grasp the handle, she saw four words written there at the edge of the door, one above the other, just at eye level.

EAT
SHIT
DIE
BOX

After a moment she pushed her way through, wiping her hands vaguely, as though they might have been contaminated by contact with the door. The words were somehow hatefully familiar. She knew she'd seen them before, and recently, but she couldn't think where it had been. Not here at the Unit, at any rate. They were probably from some song or other, of no importance or significance.

Jenny Wilcox readily accepted Aileen's offer of a drink and a lift home to Barnes. Her own car had been stolen a few weeks earlier, driven to a disused lot and set on fire, and until the insurance claim came through she was dependent on the unreliable bus service. As it was not yet opening-time, Jenny suggested that they do the drive first and go to a bar called Jewels which Jon had OK'd. This turned out to be a standard clone, like an antique shop which had started serving drinks on the side. There were lots of potted plants and brass rails and old furniture, and waitresses resembling French whores dressed as Edwardian chambermaids or vice versa flitted through the foliage. Eventually one of them was persuaded to bring the women two glasses of a Muscadet described on the blackboard wine list as 'jolly quaffable'. While they waited for it to arrive, Aileen listened to Jenny discussing her project to get all the doctors working for the local health authority to sign an advertisement naming those categories of 'non-urgent' cases whose treatment would be deferred indefinitely if funding was not increased.

'Divide and rule is the Government's game, as usual. If we let them get away with it mental health will go to the wall. To get funding you'll need publicity, which in practice means deaths. Hole-in-the-heart babies, fifteen-days-to-live kidney transplants, that sort of thing. There's no way we can compete in that market. Madness doesn't kill you, that's the trouble.'

'It can do.'

'Not directly. Anyway, from a *Daily Mail* reader's point of view, mental illness is like AIDS. Anyone who gets it had it coming to them anyway.'

Aileen said nothing. She found Jenny's ferocious cynicism hard to take in large doses, which is how it was usually administered.

'That boy I talked to you about yesterday,' she began tentatively. 'I don't suppose you've had time to observe him at all.'

'You mean what's-his-name, Gary? To tell you the truth, I haven't even noticed he's there.'

'He won't be, not after tomorrow. I haven't got anywhere with him, apart from stumbling on his real name. He's undoubtedly lying about other things too, but there's no time to discover what they are. Actually lying's not quite the right word. He seems almost to lack any clear sense of what's true and what isn't. That makes it all the more effective, of course, because there's no sense of guilt to give him away. It's as if he's holding a pack of possibilities and he deals out this one or that, according to the situation, without bothering himself about whether they happen to be true or not.'

Aileen noticed a slightly glazed look come over Jenny's eyes and realized that she was rabbiting on.

'Anyway, perhaps the police will be able to find out something about him,' she concluded.

The younger woman shot her a distinctly sharp look.

'The police?'

'I told them his real name,' Aileen explained.

'Really?'

'What's wrong with that?'

Jenny sipped her drink in silence.

'They were very nice and helpful to me when I phoned,' Aileen said defensively.

'Of course they were! You're a wealthy, middle-class, educated, white female. Why shouldn't they be nice to you? If you buy a guard dog, you don't expect it to attack *you*, do you?'

Aileen returned Jenny's look with a growing feeling of resentment.

'You're all those things too, Jenny.'

'I know I am! And I know exactly where I stand with the police, believe me.'

There was a momentary silence that was awkward in its intensity.

'Anyway, what I don't quite understand is why this particular patient matters so much to you,' Jenny went on in a more soothing tone. 'I mean concern is great, of course, but there are plenty of deserving cases at the Unit. You seem to have got very involved with this boy. What's so special about him?'

For a moment, a fraction of a second, Aileen was tempted to tell her, to open up completely and admit the mysterious and illicit identification of this boy with the ghostly child which had followed her about for over fifteen years. But she didn't. It was partly the sheer magnitude of the task that daunted her, all the painful and confusing background details she would have to relate in order to make sense of what was happening now. But she was also checked by a chilling echo of Douglas's voice in what Jenny had said. He too had asked her if she didn't think there might be a danger of her becoming too involved in her work. Aileen winced internally. Jenny Wilcox and Douglas Macklin were so different in every way that the idea of their agreeing on anything at all seemed tantamount to a proof that it must be true.

'I just can't believe that in this day and age someone can just pop up from nowhere like this,' she responded instead. 'A person with no name, no identity. I mean, I thought we were all on computers somewhere.'

'We are! The two things go together. There's a whole class of invisible people out there now, people with no name, no address, no job, no hope. Their last contact with the world we live in is by claiming social security benefits, which is one reason why the Government is making it as difficult as possible for them to do so. Because once they let go of that, they disappear totally, which is exactly what Thatcher wants. You create an underclass with no rights or privileges whatsoever and then threaten the members of the lower divisions of the social league with relegation to it if they dare complain about the lousy rights and privileges they *have* got. Just take a walk along the Embankment down by the Festival Hall some evening! Upstairs in the big glass hi-fi the bow ties and fur coats are sipping wait wain in the interval of listening to André and the RPO cream off some more of possibly-the-greatest-classics-in-the-world. Meanwhile, twenty feet below, a few hundred human derelicts are huddling up for the night in their cardboard packing cases. It's like a fucking George Grosz cartoon, except it's not Berlin in the thirties, it's London in the eighties, right here under our noses. And no one gives a *fuck*.'

'We're drinking white wine,' Aileen pointed out.

Jenny looked at her with genuine puzzlement.

'What's that got to do with it?'

But before Aileen had a chance to reply, the bar was taken over by music loud enough to make it unnecessary if not impossible. Above a synthesized beat like the clanking of an electronic dustbin lid, a choir of disembodied ghouls wailed vaguely at intervals, random bursts of demented laughter zinged about like machine-gun fire and a voice straining upwards in a manic shriek urged everyone to '*Go* for it! *Go* for it! Hup, hup, hup!' Aileen signalled for the bill, over which she and Jenny had a gentle tussle won by the younger woman.

'I just can't listen to that stuff,' Aileen commented once they were outside.

'You're not supposed to *listen* to it. It's like the background music to a film, the film of your life. You use it to add an extra dimension to the moment, to focus your style.'

'I'm just too old,' Aileen replied, putting on a slightly comic *moue* of self-deprecation.

'You're as old as you feel.'

'That's the whole trouble. I wish you only felt as old as you are. I'm not actually very old, not really, but I feel ancient. Sometimes I'm almost tempted to believe in reincarnation. It seems the only way of accounting for how tired I get. It's as if I've had many previous existences and not stayed dead long enough in between.'

Jenny's mouth opened to reveal an expanse of pink upper gum and the street echoed with her laughter.

Although the great heart-to-heart talk hadn't happened,

Aileen nevertheless felt better as she drove home. She'd had a chance to air a few of her preoccupations, at least, and the wine had made her feel pleasantly drowsy and inconsequential. The problems of the day no longer seemed quite so acute. In fact for some reason she found herself thinking about the graffiti she had seen on the door at the Unit that afternoon. She repeated the words over and over to herself as she drove along: eat, shit, die, box. They didn't seem to make any obvious sense, but there was something intriguing about them. Perhaps the last two belonged together, she mused. Could 'die-box' be a poetic formula for a coffin, like the riddling compounds in Anglo-Saxon verse? In that case the words looked like a sort of street haiku, a bleak inventory of human life. You eat, you shit, they bury you. And if you're a middle-aged childless woman, she thought, you bleed as well: uselessly, uselessly, month by month.

When Aileen parked the red Mini opposite the house, Mr Griffiths, her next-door neighbour, was at work on the tall hedge which screened his property at the front. Standing on a short step-ladder, he was busily shaving away the last of the summer growth with an electric trimmer so as to make the hedge look as much as possible like a wall. Mr Griffiths's lawn was mown so relentlessly that Aileen sometimes wondered why he didn't just replace it with artificial turf and have done. But that was to miss the point, of course. Everyone needs a hobby. Mr Griffiths's hobby was forcing Nature to play dead. They exchanged ritual greetings as Aileen passed. The nights were drawing in already, Mr Griffiths said. They were indeed, agreed Aileen. For a moment Mr Griffiths paused, regarding her with a vacuous smile as though about to venture some further confidence, perhaps to the effect that he wouldn't be surprised if there weren't a frost. But in the end he must have decided that this would be coming on a bit strong, and turned his attentions to the hedge instead.

As Aileen opened the front door, the murmur of the television revealed that Douglas was home, lapping up his daily instalment of the thinking man's soap opera.

'. . . further details as they become known. And that's the six o'clock news from the BBC. Mrs Thatcher told her critics, "We must make ourselves rich enough to be able to afford to be compassionate", and the Duchess of York made quite a splash as she became the first Royal to try out a water slide when she opened Britain's biggest-ever theme park. She said . . .'

To Aileen's surprise, however, the living room was empty. Seeing a light on, she walked across to the kitchen, but there was no sign of Douglas there either, nor a half-finished glass of Scotch on the table in the living room. Then she realized that his coat and umbrella had been missing from the rack in the hall. Her puzzlement was just beginning to turn to alarm when the phone rang.

'Yes?'

'Why don't you give the number when you answer the phone? It's no use just saying "Yes."'

'Douglas? Where are you?'

'At work. I'll be late tonight. There's a lot of things to do before I leave for Boston.'

'Douglas, the television's on, and the light in the kitchen – '

'Well, of course. They're on the automatic timer, aren't they?'

Then Aileen remembered that after the second break-in, three months earlier, Douglas had bought a complicated electronic box of tricks that switched on and off at random to simulate occupancy.

'Well, it doesn't normally happen,' she protested.

'That's because normally I get home in time to switch it off before the cycle starts. There's a button which overrides the timer. I explained all this to you when we got it.'

After he had hung up, Aileen stood quite still for a moment, feeling the house gradually expanding all around her, unfolding like a flower in the knowledge that her husband would be absent for several hours. All its spaces were open now, all the lines of tension smoothed away. She found the switch controlling the timer circuit and turned it off. Then she poured herself a glass of wine and took it upstairs to her study, which overlooked the rectangle of gardens enclosed by the houses on the adjacent streets. Overhead, the landing lights of the planes on their flight path into Heathrow were picked out against the livid grey sky, three of them in line and a fourth just turning out of the holding pattern like a star far off in the east. Douglas was flying off to Boston the next day. At the thought, the relaxed spaces of the house turned chilly. For the paradox of their relationship, the bitter truth that Aileen had finally been forced to accept, was that after twenty-four hours away from her husband she began to suffer from withdrawal symptoms, notably the most terrible depression. Without her domestic bully around, Aileen's mind started to wander. His presence increasingly drove her to distraction, but to her dismay she had found that his absence was even less bearable. Perhaps he felt something similar. That would explain why, despite everything, they had never actually broken up. There seemed to be no reason now why they shouldn't just carry on as they were, eventually turning into another old married couple, too exhausted and frightened to do each other much damage.

When she had finished her wine Aileen began to think about dinner. Only then did she realize that it was Thursday, when they normally did their weekly bulk buy, and so there would be little or nothing to eat in the house. She couldn't face going to Waitrose, so in the end she decided to pop down to the Polish delicatessen at Turnham Green and get something simple for tonight. By the time she got back it was dark. She half-expected to see Douglas's Volvo outside, but there was no sign of it. She got out of the Mini and started across the street, glancing up at the house. Aileen had never reconciled herself to the appearance of the place, quite unlike its neighbours, with fake Gothic doors and windows. The pointed arches and elaborate stone dressings, together with the slated roof and the black-painted trim, gave the place a look of hypocritical religiosity. The nearest street-lamp was some distance away, and largely screened by a large plane tree, but there was an almost full moon that night, as Aileen could have predicted from her recent insomnia. Its light silvered the path and the scrap of lawn, rendering them distinct but seemingly insubstantial.

Douglas Macklin regularly reminded his wife of her shortcomings, which included not giving the number when she answered the phone, not sheathing food in plastic before putting it in the fridge, leaving lights on and taps running, muddling his socks with hers in the wash, and slamming the front door so hard that it bounced open again. Since she had already been ticked off once that evening, Aileen was relieved that he had not come home while she was out, because when she reached the door she discovered that it was indeed open. She could just hear him say, 'It does rather tend to undermine the value of having a sophisticated timing device to deter burglars if you're going to leave the front door standing wide open, you know.' This final exaggeration was designed to lure her into protesting that the door was *not* wide open, only a crack. 'Oh, I see!' Douglas would then reply, pulling out the sixteen-foot sarcasm stop. 'Well, that's all right, then, isn't it? Perfectly safe!'

She pushed her way into the hall, set the bag of groceries down and groped for the light switch. It never ceased to surprise her that things in the dark remained where they were supposed to be, as though without the compulsion of the light they might go wandering about like untethered animals. The switch didn't work, however. Aileen flicked the lever back and forth several times, but no light appeared. Then a sudden rush of sound in the darkness at her feet startled her as the bag of shopping subsided. The bulb must have gone, she thought. Unless in turning off the automatic timer she had somehow disturbed the rest of the circuits in the house. She stood there wondering what to do, listening to the murmurs of the night. A moment ago all had seemed dead quiet, but now she discovered that what she had taken for silence was in fact a patchwork of noises: the murmur of traffic from the main road, the fridge whining in the kitchen, the gurgles of the central heating, the rustle of her breath, her rapid heartbeats. And then, somewhere upstairs, a sound that made her skin crawl.

This time she knew that it was not the water pipes. The cry was brief and not repeated, but even in that instant it was piercingly familiar. To her amazement and horror, she found herself turning towards the stairs, putting her foot on the worn patch in the centre of the lowest step. As she moved upwards like a sleep-walker, the dimness of the hallway gradually closed up until it was wholly dark. Beyond the local clamour of the stairs and her thumping heart, all seemed silent, crouched and waiting. She was well aware that what she was doing was absolute madness, but she had no choice.

She continued to climb, one hand held out in front of her, until her groping foot could feel no further step. She could now see nothing, but knew she must be standing on the landing. Gradually her breath grew steadier and she felt her body relax. The reality of the sound she had heard began to grow abstract and doubtful. It *must* have been the pipes, she thought. What else could it have been? There was no baby in the house. Then a door opened and the accumulated darkness gathered itself up and rushed her. She was gripped by a terror so great that she could do nothing but stand there, trembling and ready to vomit, as it went barging past, sending her reeling backwards down the stairs, head over heels in a gradual graceless slither.

When she sat up, the front door was fully open and the hallway calmly illuminated by the moonlight. She crawled over to the phone and punched the numbered buttons. Only when Douglas came on the line, inquiring rather curtly what she wanted, only then, absurdly enough, did she begin to scream.

EIGHT

Steve looked forward to his shopping expeditions for the old man. Apart from his trips to the OOD S ORE, they provided his only chance to take part in the real business of life, the thing that made sense of it all. Until then he'd been a mere spectator, wandering through the covered mall where the shops spilt out on to the promenade and the goods were heaped up in seemingly wanton profusion. It looked as though there was more than enough for everyone, as though you could just help yourself, but of course these free and easy manners were only a tease. The gorgeous hordes of goodies had their pimps, big ugly toughs in cheapo uniforms with spluttering walkie-talkies who sized up the punters' spending power at a glance. If you looked too lingeringly at the merchandise or fondled it with too much feeling, without having what it took to take it home, then they moved in fast.

Nevertheless, the boy sometimes used to risk loading up a trolley with items, pretending to think long and hard about some, chucking others carelessly in, just like the shoppers whose mannerisms he had studied. The prices were already familiar to him. The stotters never missed an episode of the television show where people won things by knowing how much they cost. 'Stupid *cow*!' Jimmy would jeer. 'Three hundred and ninety-nine quid? Up my arse!' But when the trolley was full Steve had to abandon it and slip away empty-handed, so it was poor fun compared to the real thing. Besides, interpreting the old man's lists involved a satisfying degree of responsibility. The instructions ranged from the nebulous ('Vegetables. Fruit?') to the pedantic ('Steak and kidney pudding, *not* pie – Fray Bentos if possible, otherwise a small one only'). This kept Steve on his toes, and he prided himself on being able to account for every penny he spent.

But there was another and deeper reason for the boy's satisfaction. Ever since the time when his collection of snapshot memories had been taken, he had been surrounded by people whose job was to look after him. However kind they were, he could never forget that they were *paid* to care. They fed and clothed and sheltered him because doing so provided their own food, clothes and shelter. They were really caring for themselves, not him at all. Of course there might be something else there, something real, but you could never prove it. Sometimes the other boys tried to do so by acting impossible, smashing the place up or trying to kill themselves, but what good was that? If the social workers and house parents continued to accept you however badly you behaved, it just proved how badly they needed the money. Steve felt sorry for these official minders, their lives made a misery by little shits like him. *He* wouldn't have done their job, not for anything.

What had attracted him to the stotters was that they'd taken him on of their own free will. At the same time he knew it had really been a freak, a whim which had briefly flared in the darkness of Jimmy's brain and which he'd imposed on the others in a fit of pique. Besides, they never allowed Steve to forget that he was dependent on them, a household pet who would be abandoned the moment they lost interest in him. With the old man it was different. The old man *needed* him. Again, there were moments when Steve wondered if perhaps there was more to it than that, love or whatever it was called. But the boy knew that you couldn't build on anything as vague and feeble as that. Need was the stuff, need you could count on. He still didn't understand what created Ernest Matthews's need, why he couldn't just go out and do things for himself like everyone else. Presumably it had something to do with the man Steve had nicknamed Hazchem. The story the old man was telling him would make all that clear. In any case, it wasn't important. All that mattered was the need itself. It was as real as money: warm and smelling of people, of their dirt and their weakness. And Steve had a pocketful of it!

Friday being pay-day, all the tills at the checkout were busy. The trolleys lined up one behind the other, piled high with sliced white, washing powder, baked beans, ice cream, dog food and toilet rolls. Stunned-looking men with tattooed biceps and soft tummies stood awkwardly beside women in whose faces beauty came and went like the picture on a poorly tuned television set. Both sexes looked prematurely old, exhausted and bewildered, casualties of some routine disaster. Around their legs children clung and stumbled, their faces smudged with bruises, red with tears, cuts below their eyes.

Some one pushed Steve roughly from behind.

'Fuck you doing here?'

It was Dave and wee Alex, with a trolley full of cans of lager. Dave gave the boy an even more meaningful punch.

'Asked you a question, wanker!'

'Shopping,' Steve said.

Dave pawed through the contents of his basket.

'Who's this shit for? Where you get the money, you little fucker?'

'Robbing Peter to pay Paul,' muttered Alex.

'It's for this old bloke,' Steve explained. 'He can't get out. He's crippled.'

'*You'll* be fucking crippled, time I've finished with you,' Dave snapped.

At that moment the security guard intervened. A huge West Indian who never stopped smiling, he looked like a black Santa Claus.

'Now then, lads, let's calm down,' he said in a voice that seemed to come from somewhere beneath the floor. He was still smiling merrily. Dave backed away, scowling.

'They giving you any trouble?' the guard asked Steve.

'No, it's all right. I know them.'

The guard moved away, but not very far. He kept an eye on the trio while Steve unloaded his basket and paid, under Dave's and Alex's hostile scrutiny. When he had packed the shopping into the orange sling, the boy walked quickly to the door without looking back. Once outside he started to run. His plan was to make it as far as the public lavatory by the park and hide in the cubicle with the broken window. It was only a temporary respite, of course. They'd get him when he came home. But at least it would give Dave a chance to cool down a little. The shopping was heavy and awkward to run with, but Steve hurried on as best he could. When he reached the lavatory, he stopped and looked round. There was no sign of Dave and Alex. They probably hadn't even bothered to try to catch him. Steve always tended to overestimate the stotters' energy. He slipped inside and sat down in his favourite cublicle.

The story on which his eye usually fell first, because of its position, was so squeezed in that the final words of each line had been pushed up on to the door frame. The story itself Steve found particularly obscure, since it lacked the usual terms for the parts of the body and the things people did with them. It began 'THIS SCHOOLGIRL ASKED ME TO EAT HER OUT FIRST I LICKED HER LITTLE BUSH IT FELT SO GOOD I THOUGHT I WOULD DIE SO SHE BEGGED ME TO STICK MY TONGUE DEEP IN HER BOX AND I DID IT TASTED LIKE HEAVEN', after which the writing became increasingly vertical and eventually slipped off the wall altogether in a rather pedestrian ending including such details as the fact that the schoolgirl in question was only thirteen and came there every week looking for older men. Steve leant back, the downpipe of the toilet pressing against his back like a second spinal column, trying to work out what the story was about. It seemed to involve a meal the writer had had with someone he loved, but the details escaped him.

When Steve came out of the lavatory it had started to drizzle. He hurried on along Paxton Grove, half-walking and half-running over the cracked uneven slabs. The house in Grafton Avenue seemed cosier and safer and more welcoming than ever that day. Ernest Matthews's high tea the week before had been such a success that the old man had decided to make it a regular event. The water was already bubbling in an enamel saucepan on the stove, and while Steve unpacked and put away the rest of the shopping Matthews lowered the eggs in one by one, tut-tutting when one of them cracked, releasing a milky cloud. He stood in front of the stove, watch in hand like a station-master, until the statutory three minutes had elapsed. Then the eggs were promptly rushed to the table, where Steve demonstrated that he had mastered the art of opening them correctly. Then they ate, soaking up the runny yolk with strips of buttered bread before taking up their spoons to excavate the white.

Afterwards, as Steve sat looking round at the sideboard laden with nameless oddities, he realized for the first time what made this room feel so special, so different from any other: you couldn't have won anything in it on that television game show. Steve had always assumed that everything had a price the same way it had a name. But the old man's room was full of things that had neither. They seemed to have sprung magically out of nowhere, their very existence a scandal.

'Where you get all this stuff?' the boy demanded finally.

'It was here before I came. All in different rooms, scattered throughout the house. I brought it all in here, what I wanted. Some of it was my mother's, you see.'

But for some reason Steve didn't want to see.

'When you going to get on with the story?' he asked, glancing pointedly at the clock.

'My, but we're impatient today!' Matthews remarked. 'Very well, then. Where were we?'

'Hiding behind the hedge listening to the man telling his friend about the woman he'd seen,' the boy promptly replied. The fact that he didn't believe the old man's tale actually made it easier for him to remember, just as the things that he and the stotters watched on TV always seemed more real than what happened in between.

Ernest Matthews nodded and smiled, pleased that the boy had not forgotten.

'Good lad! That's it. That's it exactly. Well, as I said, Maurice Jeffries went on and on about this young woman he claimed to have seen on the lawn in the middle of the night, how she was the woman of his dreams, the woman he'd been hoping to meet one day. In fact he started getting so carried away that I began to wonder whether he was quite right in the head. Nor was I the only one, for Aubrey Deville, the friend to whom he was telling all this, started chaffing him about it. But Maurice refused to make a joke of it. He became more and more impassioned, until Deville hastily assured him that he believed every word he said and would watch with him that night, prepared to follow the woman if she should appear. That's as much as I heard, for just then the head gardener appeared and started giving me what for. But though I went back to work hoeing the flowers, it wasn't *that* bed I was thinking about for the rest of the afternoon, I can assure you. For when I heard Maurice describing this ravishing female roaming around the garden in her shift in the middle of the night, it was as though I could actually see her in front of me, and not exactly overdressed for the time of year, if you know what I mean.'

He paused, giving Steve a sideways glance.

'*Do* you know what I mean?'

The boy thought about Tracy. Sometimes at night, to help get to sleep, he would tell himself a story in which he and Tracy were alone in the house, the stotters having conveniently disappeared. In the story, he heard footsteps, soft and quiet, bare feet coming towards him across the floorboards. Then the mattress would dip unexpectedly and it was her, Tracy, lying down beside him, explaining that she felt cold and lonely and afraid too. Close together, their bodies made heat instead of losing it. She turned around so that her fine smooth back fitted snugly into the hollow of his chest, his knees pressed into the sockets at the back of hers, and he would lick that supple hollow where shoulder moulded into neck. 'You're more beautiful than Hammersmith Bridge,' he would murmur.

Sensing that he had lost his audience, the old man gave a theatrical cough.

'Well, that's neither here nor there,' he said. 'But it so happens that at the time of which I'm speaking, I had got friendly with one of the housemaids, name of Elsie. The female staff slept in the attic rooms, where they were locked in at night. But love will ever find a way, and I'd soon found mine up through a trapdoor on to the roof, which was almost flat. Once there, I had the run of the whole length of the Hall, and it was no great difficulty for an agile lad like myself to shin down a drainpipe and in through Elsie's window. Anyway, that afternoon, thinking over what Maurice had said, it occurred to me that I too could stay up and watch for the woman he had described. I even wondered if I might not be able to solve the riddle that so perplexed Maurice. ''Who is she?'' he'd asked Aubrey Deville. ''Who can she be?'' Well, I knew the area better than the young master, and everyone who lived there was familiar to me. If the woman came, I thought, then I would recognize her.

'As soon as the house was quiet that night I made my way up through the trapdoor and out on to the leads of the roof. It was a mild summer night. The sky was hazy, and the moon sat behind it as plump as a lantern. I made my way carefully along the roof to the west wing, from which I had a good view over the lawn and the main part of the house, where Maurice had his rooms. All the windows were dark. To my right, the lawn lay as smooth as a billiard table, with the two beech trees that rose taller than the house itself. Behind them I could just make out the fence where the park began, and the dark swell of the hillside beyond. On the other side lay the river and the railway, while up the valley to the west I could make out the roofs of the village, all silvery in the moonlight. Now you mustn't suppose that anything happened right away. It never does, you know, except in stories. To pass the time, and maybe to steady myself, for it was a little spooky up there all alone on the roof at night, I started to go the rounds of each house in the village, in my thoughts I mean, flitting from one cottage to the next like a ghost. I knew them all, you see. I made my way from one to the next, opening doors and moving from room to room, pausing to gaze down at the people asleep in bed. I felt solemn and sad, although at the time I didn't understand why. The only sound throughout was the hushing of the river, and after I had finished with the village, I began to follow it downstream in my thoughts, past the farms and meadows I'd grown up with, then to the local market town and beyond, the river growing larger and smoother and more stately all the time, until it reached the metropolis and then the ocean that spanned the entire globe, patrolled by our warships and policed by our troops. It was peaceful and yet thrilling to lie there listening to the murmur of that tiny stream, and know that those drops of water were one with those that lapped the shores of Africa and India, Australia and the East, fabulous places where at that very moment the sun was just rising or was already high in the sky.

'At any rate, nothing occured to draw me from these reveries. The church clock told off the hours one after the other, until I began to consider how tired I would be in the morning and wonder if I shouldn't go to bed while there was still time. It had struck four when I heard a sliding creaking sound which brought me bolt upright in an instant. Looking down at the face of the house, I saw that the lower sash of one window had been thrown up. Someone was looking towards the lawn, and I heard Maurice's voice calling, "Who are you? Where are you going?" But to my bitter disappointment, when I looked towards the lawn there was nothing whatever to be seen. I had good eyes in those days, and from my perch on the roof I could see the whole extent of the garden as clear as day, but there was nothing there. No mysterious figures in nightdresses, no movement, no glimmers, nothing. When I looked back at the house, Maurice had disappeared from the window. A few moments later I heard a series of noises down below, and then the front door of the Hall opened and I saw something that capped my growing sense of the madness of the scene. Unlike his brother Rupert, who took all nature for his drawing room, Maurice would hardly venture out of the house from one day's end to the next, as I told you. Nevertheless, there he was now, at a quarter past four in the morning, running towards me across the lawn and into the shrubbery below, where I lost sight of him, although I heard his footsteps a while longer on the path leading to the stables and the church. I quickly made my way back along the roof to the trapdoor and scuttled down the back stairs to the servants' quarters. I let myself out through the scullery window and hurried around to the end of the west wing, where I stopped to make sure that I was not observed, for my next step would have taken me out into the open.

'A heavy dew had come down, and the moonlight sparkled from each drop on every blade of grass, making a smooth sheet of shimmering light that looked more like a lake than a lawn. What I saw there stopped me going any further. For that shining surface was broken by a single line of footprints stretching back across it like spots of candlewax on polished floorboards. Close to the house they divided in two, one set leading to the front door and the other to a door in the east wing, opposite to where I was standing. The message I read there seemed pretty plain to me. In the time it had taken me to climb down from the roof, get out through the scullery window and run round to the front of the house, Maurice Jeffries had thought better of the advisability of roaming about the grounds in the middle of the night and had returned to the house. And what had finally made him see the error of his ways, I thought, might perhaps have been the same thing that convinced me that I had been wasting my time. For it would have been impossible for any human being to have crossed the lawn that night without breaking the luminous sheet of dew that lay upon it, and yet the only footprints quite clearly led to and from the house. That clinched it. The mysterious apparition Maurice claimed to have seen had no existence outside his own head, in which case that head must be addled. And in that case, I thought as I made my way back to the scullery window, Maurice will be locked up in an asylum, Rupert will become sole master of the estate and we need have no more fears for the future.

'The next day I felt as weak and dreamy as a girl, and I paid little enough attention when I heard that Maurice was nowhere to be found. He had always been subject to sudden whims and flights of fancy, and was famous for doing whatever came into his head without taking the least trouble to consult anyone else's convenience. Nevertheless, this disappearance was bizarre even by his standards, for his clothes and personal belongings were all in his room, and even his valet knew nothing of his whereabouts. But I said nothing about what I'd seen during my night on the roof, for whatever happened to anyone else, I should have been severely punished. Besides, it was not for me but Aubrey Deville, if he chose, to divulge the tale which Maurice had told him in strict confidence. As he said nothing, I felt no qualms about remaining silent. As for Maurice's mysterious lady friend, no more was ever heard of her, and a few weeks later the whole episode was forgotten, for we were at war.'

Ernest Matthews glanced at Steve, who was leaning forward attentively.

'There you are!' the old man exclaimed. 'You're interested now, aren't you? Actions speak louder than words, they say, but there are some words that speak loud enough for anything , and one of them is war. Once it had been spoken, Maurice's disappearance came to seem of little account, particularly since his brother hinted that the two events were not entirely unconnected. Rupert had argued all along that a big European war was what was needed to get the country trim and fit again. Nor was he the only person to think like that. Of course, no one doubted that if war came, we would win with ease. The whole thing would be over by Christmas at the latest, after which the old life would pick up again just the same as before, except that we'd all be healthier and more robust for the exercise. That was most people's view, but Maurice thought very differently. He used to say that a war would ruin everything. "The country just now is like a play at the end of the second act," he said. "There is an interesting cast and the plot is developing splendidly. But if war comes, all that will go for nothing. We'll be left with a botched job, a work of genius completed by a hack." Needless to say, Rupert took a less flattering view of his brother's pacifism. "If Maurice has chosen this particular moment to vanish from view," he said, "then I for one have no desire to interfere. The glorious sacrifice which we may all be called upon to make loses its meaning unless it is freely offered, and the duties which my brother has sought to demean are honourable only if undertaken in a spirit of glad comradeship." Rupert himself enlisted immediately war broke out.

'But the war *wasn't* over by Christmas, nor by the one after that, by which time our army had been knocked about so much that they decided they needed a new one. There was no difficulty finding volunteers. Everyone had heard what monsters the enemy were and we couldn't wait to go and settle accounts with them. I myself was wild to enlist, but you had to be nineteen, which left me three years short. Then one day I met a boy I knew from the village, swaggering along as pleased as Punch. "You look like the cat that got the cream," I says. "I must bid you farewell," he says to me, as solemn as the vicar, "for I'm off to France in the morning to fight for my king and country." The impudence of it! I was thunderstruck. Him, a boy scarcely a year older than me, giving himself the airs of a national hero, a martyr! "You're no more nineteen than I am!" I cried. "That's not what the Army thinks," says he. And with that he told me how at first when they asked him how old he was he'd said seventeen. " 'Minimum age nineteen years, lad,' the sergeant replies. 'Now then, I'm a bit deaf on that side,' he says with a broad wink, 'and I didn't quite catch your age. Let me have it in the other ear.' " So this time of course he says nineteen and they let him in. Well, the very next day I begged a ride to town on the carrier's cart, went down to the recruiting office and told them the same story as impudently as I could manage. Much to my surprise, I walked out of there half an hour later Private Ernest Matthews, the newest member of the New Army. When we were all sent off to training camp a few weeks later, the whole village was there to see us off. We felt like conquering heroes! I was sad to leave my mother in tears, but despite what happened afterwards, I have to say that that was the happiest and most exciting day of my life.

'As soon as we were trained, they sent us over to France. The other lads were jolly and chummy. We might have been going on holiday. Once across the Channel, we were put on a slow train that crawled through the countryside for what seemed an eternity. At last it stopped, in the middle of nowhere, and we were ordered out and set to march all day and most of the night until we reached our camp. The whole place was in chaos with preparations for the offensive, thousands of people and mounds of equipment coming and going and the guns pounding continually like the end of the world was at hand. But absurd as it may seem, the only thing that worried me at the time was the possibility of being found out by Rupert Jeffries. Everyone from our part of the country was in the same battalion, you see, so I knew I'd see him sooner or later, and of course he knew my real age well enough. I was afraid he might have me disciplined, or even sent home in disgrace. But when he finally saw me, a few days after we arrived, he merely grinned, patted my shoulder and called me a brave lad.

'As I said, there was a big attack in preparation, so big that everyone supposed that it would put an end to the war. It was just a few days before it began that we heard the news about Maurice. Even before I left home, the countryside had been transformed. We couldn't bring in all our wheat from the Empire any more, you see, so the land which had been lying fallow since the bad days of the seventies was all ploughed up again, and they even started to clear what remained of the forest as well. It was in that way that Maurice's fate came to light. The land around the Hall had once been covered with a great forest stretching for miles in every direction. Some old men could still remember when it had surrounded the village like a sea, but little by little it had been broken up and thinned out until there was just the one big patch left, forming a hanger on the wolds above the Hall. In the midst of it was an old house that had once been a hunting lodge, which everyone called the trysting-house.'

He shot a glance in Steve's direction.

'I don't suppose you know what a tryst is? It's a meeting, an arrangement between two sweethearts. What they call a "rendezvous" nowadays, as though we hadn't a good enough word in plain English. This house had been standing empty for years, and courting couples used it when they wanted to be alone, which was no easy thing in those days. It was a fine house, too, built of the local stone, three storeys high, with big gables. The garden was a waste of weeds and stinging-nettles, with a yew tree grown so wild it almost hid the house, though with the wood so close the place was always dark enough. I was scared to go there, to tell you the truth, even with the other lads. Partly it was the folk who lived in the woods. They were farm labourers who had been turned out of their homes when the bad times came and had been living up there like gypsies ever since. But it was also the place itself. It used to give me the shivers, I don't know why. At any rate, the forest had all been chopped down now. They'd felled the tall beeches and were grubbing out the undergrowth close to the house when they came upon a shallow grave in which the body of Maurice Jeffries lay buried, his skull crushed in and every bone in his body broken.'

Ernest Matthews looked at Steve and frowned.

'But you're not listening,' he complained.

The boy started.

'It's my own fault,' the old man mused sadly, tapping the ashes of his pipe. 'I've gone on too long. Look, it's gone six. You'd better be off.'

It was spoken curtly, almost an order. Steve rose unwillingly. It was a joke, the old man thinking that he was in a hurry to leave. On the contrary, what was distracting him was precisely the fear of what awaited him on his return to Trencham Avenue. He knew that Dave would make him pay for having witnessed his humiliation by the security guard, while Jimmy would want to know who the shopping was for and why he hadn't been told about it earlier. He was going to get it, that much was certain. Since he had decided not to tell them any more about the old man, he was going to have to think up a story. He hoped that Dave wouldn't hurt him too badly, that one of the others would pull him off before he lost control.

NINE

When Aileen was called out of the ward meeting on Friday morning and told that the police wanted to speak to her on the phone, she knew instinctively that Douglas's plane had crashed. She had spent much of the night lying sleepless at her husband's side, not daring to move lest she wake him, thinking about what had happened that evening, trying to come to terms with it, to analyse what had been so disturbing about the event. In fact they had got off relatively lightly this time. The last time that their house had been broken into the living room had been reduced to an utter shambles: pictures smashed, cupboards staved in, ornaments mutilated, photographs torn up, books ripped apart, sofa and chairs slashed, the curtains cut to ribbons, the carpet burned and the wallpaper smeared with excrement. 'Amateurs, probably kids from the council estate,' the police had said off-handedly. 'Broke in through the garden windows then couldn't get past the locked door to the hallway. Never lock internal doors, it just winds them up.' That experience had changed Aileen's view of the place where she lived. The house felt scarred and vulnerable, the street at risk, its genteel façade a shabby deceit. The whole area had revealed itself to be psychotic.

But at least she hadn't had to face the intruders herself, although every time she passed the youngsters playing in the car-park of the council flats nearby, she wondered if some of them had done it. The break-in itself had to some extent remained distanced by its anonymity, like one of those things you read about in the papers or hear discussed at a dinner party. The personal touch had been lacking. But not this time, she thought, recalling that brief unimaginably intense scuffle on the landing, a physical encounter as shockingly intimate as her early sexual gropings, thrilling and horrid. Of course she hadn't dreamt of discussing this with Douglas, any more than she had mentioned the thing that had started it all, although the memory of it still made her shiver all over: the baby's cry shining eerily out of the silence, drawing her helplessly towards it. When Douglas had arrived with the police – in a very bad temper because not only had his last-minute arrangements been disturbed but in the circumstances he couldn't very well blame Aileen for it – they had searched the house. No damage had been done and relatively little was missing. The burglar, who had also broken in through the garden window, leaving the front door open for a speedy departure, had clearly been a professional. He had probably spent several weeks watching the street, and having established that the Macklins went to the supermarket on Thursdays he thought he had a clear hour or so to go through the house thoroughly. Aileen's prompt return had disturbed him while he was investigating her jewellery. On the dressing-table stood a large doll dating from her childhood and now retained as an ornament. When it was moved, a mechanism inside emitted a crying sound.

Oddly enough, the knowledge that this was all it had been did nothing to calm Aileen's agitation. Too much primal goo had been dredged up from the depths. The doll's cry was not even particularly realistic, and although its connection with her childhood no doubt lent the sound emotional force, Aileen was only too aware that the experience had drawn most of its power from the events that had followed Raymond's death. Lying tormentedly still in the constrained intimacy of the conjugal bed, she thought about the flashback experiences which some people reportedly had years after taking LSD, when for no apparent reason they would suddenly find themselves high again, the ground blurring away beneath them and the people around looking strange. It was almost as if something of the sort was happening to her. I'm no longer in full control of my life, she thought. A pattern has been indelibly engraved on my psyche and I perceive everything that happens to me in terms of that pattern. Which is madness, she concluded, proving her sanity with a joke.

The morning that followed had not helped to restore her equilibrium. As always when he went away, Douglas was in a foul mood, tense and snappy. Knowing that his wife was nervous about him flying, he taunted her with statistics which suggested that boarding an airplane was less dangerous than walking upstairs in one's own house. Aileen said nothing. She drove Douglas and his fibre-glass suitcase – the manufacturer's claims suggested that *it* would survive whatever happened – to Hammersmith tube and waved goodbye with a hollowly casual, 'See you on Monday, then.' But when one of the secretaries interrupted the discussion on the therapeutic merits of projective techniques to tell Aileen that she was wanted on the phone by the police, she felt her insides give a sickening lurch, as when you drive too fast over a hump-backed bridge, and she knew at once what had happened. It was then almost one o'clock. Douglas's flight had left at eleven. It would have taken time to get hold of the passenger list, and they would first have called the Institute and then the Macklins' home number. Aileen had a sudden vision of the slim white phone, like overlapping lovers' hands, chirping plaintively to an empty house. As she followed the secretary along the corridor, the linoleum squelching like mud under her soles, her only real surprise was that the police hadn't come to break the news in person. The last time, they'd sent a pair of rookies, callow insolent punks whose veneer of sorrowful concern swiftly peeled off as they looked round, taking in the colourful, indiscriminate, organic mess, the smell of dope and incense, the Dayglo posters and anti-war slogans, the books on Buddhism and vegetarian cookery, the endlessly repeated riff booming from the stereo where a record no one was listening to had got stuck in a groove. But, of course, Raymond's had been just a single death. There would have been three or four hundred people on the flight to Boston: they couldn't possibly inform all the next-of-kin personally.

'Aileen Macklin speaking.'

'Hello and good morning, Hammersmith CID, Detective Inspector Croom. I am calling pursuant to the matter on which you were in communication relative to one Steven Bradley.'

For a moment Aileen felt too surprised to speak.

'Have you . . . have you found out something, then?' she finally managed.

'We certainly have, madam. In fact it would not be too much to infer that we've found out *everything*. Who he is, where he comes from, the works. Gary Dunn didn't mean nothing to us, but Steven Bradley, well, that was different. Not to put too fine a point on it, we've been able to wrap up an assortment of unsolved cases, comprising of two murders, two GBH, and a string of assorted robbery with threat, uttering menaces, aiding and abetting, not to mention the odd taking and driving away and anything else they may ask to be taken into consideration.'

Aileen gripped the receiver tightly, forcing herself to concentrate.

'What has this got to do with Gary – I mean Steven?'

'Well, that's a bit complicated, to say the least. I can't enter into it on the phone, anyway. If you could pop down the station for half an hour some time, say late morning or early afternoon, I or one of my colleagues will be more than happy to map out the situation with regard to this one.'

Aileen agreed hastily and hung up. So Douglas wasn't dead. How odd. Not that the call hadn't been about that, of course. It was her conviction that it *had* that was odd, or worse than odd. It was bad enough to wish your husband dead. When you started believing that your wishes had come true, you were in real trouble. Was she really losing that instinctive sense of balance which all sane people have without knowing it, but which is so hard to define and even harder to get or give back once it has gone? If so, it was all Douglas's fault. he had been trying for years to drive her mad, and now – racked by sleeplessness, worry and doubt – Aileen was prepared to admit for the first time that he might be succeeding. She had been proud of her ability to hold her own in their daily battles, too proud to realize that she should never have agreed to take part in the first place. For the rules of that domestic warfare had been drawn up by her husband, and although Aileen had proved herself remarkably adept, she still had to force herself to do what came naturally to him. His defeats hardly troubled him, but she suffered even when she won. The continual separation of her thoughts into those that were admissible and inadmissible had become second nature to her, and the price she had paid was an equivalent separation within herself, a loss of wholeness. The essential question for her was no longer 'Is this really what I think or feel?' but 'If I admit to thinking or feeling this, will he be able to use it against me?' Her true motives and reactions had come to represent a danger to her, potential weaknesses that her husband would attack if he suspected their existence. After so many years of painfully carrying on an adulterous relationship with reality, it looked as though she had finally decided to break off the affair. It just didn't seem worth the bother any more.

When Aileen got back to her office at lunch-time, the communicating door was open. Through it she could see Jenny Wilcox, dressed in a blue leotard. The occupational therapist's heels were leaning on the top of a filing cabinet. Her head rested on the floor, cushioned by the E–K telephone directory.

'Meeting of the action group this afternoon,' she remarked in a voice constrained by the weight of her body. 'Hope you can make it. It's a bums-on-seats situation.'

Aileen dumped her files and folders on the desk and grunted ambiguously. After a while Jenny lowered her legs to the ground and sat up.

'What's wrong?' she exclaimed. 'You look like death warmed up.'

'I think I'm going mad.'

Jenny grasped her right foot and leant forward, stretching her back.

'Join the club. Any special reason, apart from living in Thatcher's Britain?'

Aileen unwrapped her lunch, a cheese roll and a plastic pot filled with the raw vegetable that Douglas, laboriously whimsical, referred to as 'raped carrot'.

'Someone broke into the house last night. I'd just popped down to get something from the shops. When I got back he was still there. It gave me quite a turn.'

Jenny switched her attentions to the other foot.

'Did you nail him?'

'Not really. He rather sort of nailed me, actually.'

'You should have done that self-defence course I told you about. I mean, you were *lucky*. I wish I'd had a chance to confront the fuckers who trashed my Fiat. Talk about a short sharp shock!'

Aileen sat looking without enthusiasm at her food. What she really wanted was a cigarette. Jenny's comments had once again brought her up short against the disconcerting fact that political opinions apart, the younger woman's character was that of her class, the service aristocracy, which once provided the nation with its officers, diplomats and explorers. Jenny had no patience with people who couldn't cope. In that, despite the yawning gulf in ideology, she resembled the Cheltenham schoolmates whom Aileen bumped into occasionally and who always managed to leave her feeling spineless and incompetent. No doubt this bracing manner had a lot to commend it, but Aileen didn't feel like being braced just then. Ironically, although she had a perfect excuse for getting away, she couldn't use it with Jenny for fear of being criticized for collaborating with the police. As so often, a plausible fiction was the answer.

'I must run, Jenny. I have to take the Mini to the garage. The brakes have been giving trouble.'

The driveway to the Unit was blocked by a delivery lorry, which was trying to reverse into the unloading bay by the kitchen. As she waited, Aileen thought about the unexpected breakthrough that had apparently resulted from her discovery of the boy's real name. Full marks, she told herself. Give yourself credit where credit is due. Not everything was going to pieces. Despite the almost intolerable pressures on her over the last week, she had done her job. 'We've found out everything,' the policeman had said. 'Who he is, where he comes from, the works.' Armed with that information, Aileen was confident that the boy's treatment could be adequately undertaken on a day-patient basis. It only remained to sell that idea to Steven himself, which she would do first thing that afternoon, before Pamela Haynes came to pick him up and drive him to the hostel where he was being housed until a permanent home could be found for him.

Aileen tapped the steering wheel impatiently. She felt cold, having been misled by another fine morning into putting on a thin white sleeveless cotton dress which had proved totally inadequate once the clouds rolled up. Besides, it was getting late. Someone had thoughtlessly parked in such a way that it was almost impossible for the lorry to get into the space reserved for it. In the end Aileen did a three-point turn and drove along the link road to the main psychiatric hospital. At the front of that forbidding edifice she slowed to go over the speed bump. To the left, incongruously tacked on to the Victorian redbrick, was a compound full of storage cylinders and a mass of silver tubing. The wire fence that surrounded it was marked 'WARNING HAZCHEM'. The words reminded Aileen of something someone had said to her recently. But as usual these days, she couldn't for the life of her remember who it had been or why it had stuck in her mind. Despite its exotic appearance, the sign merely indicated the presence of hazardous chemicals, in this case the various explosive or inflammable substances used in the hospital. As she accelerated down the driveway to the street, Aileen recalled that Douglas liked to define the human brain as a bowl of chemical soup. In that case, she thought, perhaps we should all wear a sign like the one on that wire fence. For one thing that was certain was that those chemicals, too, were hazardous.

TEN

Uneasy hints of spring struggled against the wintry dusk like a river running feebly against the incoming tide. At the corner where Steve turned out of the main road, two men and two women were standing around an empty pushchair. The boy mechanically noted the tell-tale signs of impairment: the bodies swaying back and forth like plants in the wind, feet continually shuffling to maintain balance, the rigid tunnel-vision gaze, the blurred voices all spluttering away at the same time. The two men were grasping cans of Carlsberg Special Brew. One of the women was holding a baby in her arms while the other lit a cigarette. The quartet kept up a constant patter, a verbal scaffolding on which they leant, tilting in towards each other.

'. . . do for him . . .'

'. . . little darling . . .'

'. . . wants he wants . . .'

'. . . bet your life . . .'

'. . . just the job . . .'

'. . . little pet . . .'

'. . . right as rain . . .'

'. . . never worry . . .'

One of the men took a feeding-bottle from the pushchair and poured beer into it. The two women, feinting and weaving like wrestlers, were trying to pass the baby from one pair of outstretched hands to another. The shopping hurt Steve's shoulder, which still ached from the beating he'd received the week before, but he was determined to keep going until he reached the public lavatory. There he could not only have a rest but also put to use the pen he'd bought out of the money the old man allowed him. The stotters wouldn't be getting it any more, not after what they'd done to him. Dave and Alex had started in as soon as he got home. Jimmy hadn't been there, and if it hadn't been for Tracy, Steve was sure they'd have killed him. They'd stood at either side of the room, tossing the boy back and forth between them, but instead of catching him, they'd stuck out their knees or elbows or fists or stood aside at the last moment and let him hit the floor or the wall before kicking him to his feet again. His helplessness had excited them and they went about their work with grunts and squeals, like when they were labouring over Tracy late at night.

The worst of it had been their silence. Steve had expected angry questions which he would somehow satisfy, making up versions of the truth good enough for people who could hardly remember their own names half the time. But they hadn't asked any questions. They had just hurled him about until he lost all sense of time and place, of who he was and who they were and why this was happening. Once the stotters got started on something, fucking or fighting or whatever it might be, it was almost impossible for them to stop unless someone came along and switched them off. That was normally Steve's task, but now he had fallen into the machine himself, and it was slowly but surely beating him to a pulp. There was nothing personal about it. That was the whole problem. Dave and Alex couldn't have stopped even if they'd wanted to. They wouldn't have known how.

In the end he had been saved, though, and by Tracy, which almost made it worthwhile. After screaming at the two men in vain for some time, she'd eventually thrown herself on Steve, wrestling him to the ground and daring Dave and Alex to come and take him back. But they didn't even try. They just stood looking about them with bewildered expressions, like children whose favourite toy has been snatched away. Then Alex turned on the television, Dave cracked open another can of lager and a few minutes later they had forgotten all about it.

But Steve didn't forget, and during the week that followed he decided that the time had come to celebrate his feelings for Tracy publicly. If it hadn't been for her he would have left, taken his chances sleeping rough again, or perhaps even asked the old man if he could stay there. But he felt that he had to stand by Tracy, ready to protect her as she had protected him, deflecting the stotters' moods, playing them off against each other, managing them without their being aware of it. Steve saw it as a bond between them, and although they had never spoken about it, he was sure Tracy considered him her friend and ally.

Sometimes, despite his caution, she caught him looking at her, and then the look she gave him was so dense and heady, so charged with meaning, that it seemed to make words both impossible and unnecessary. So the following week Steve added a felt-tipped pen to his shopping list, and on the way back to Grafton Avenue he stopped at the lavatory to share his feelings about the person he loved. He didn't yet know what he was going to say, although he knew that it would be different from the other stories on those closely covered walls. Steve was not interested in Tracy's underwear or shoes, and there was certainly no point in imagining her carrying on like the women in the other stories: he saw all that at home just about every evening. In any case, that had nothing to do with love, so he'd just skip it, the way the other writers skipped the bits that didn't interest them, and get straight to the point: the warmth, the tenderness, the cuddles, the love that grew stronger and stronger until it could hold the whole world at bay.

The moment he passed through the doorless portal, Steve knew that something strange and sinister had occurred. The building was bare, stripped and featureless. Even the familiar smells had been usurped by an alien odour. As for the walls, the change was almost too much to take in at first. The stories were gone! All those tightly organized patches and clusters of writing had been brutally erased, all that concentrated passion and pain diluted by powerful industrial solvents to a thin grey film smeared over the basic beige. Steve groped his way to the cubicle with the broken window and collapsed, his head in his hands and tears running down his cheeks. How could they do such a thing? Those stories were like friends to him, as reassuring and predictable as the doors he'd got to know on his newspaper round; individual and interesting, yet perfectly safe. Any time he happened to be passing he could drop in and visit them. And now some faceless fucker in a wanker's uniform had come along and said they had no right to be there! It was too cruel, worse than any pain the stotters had been able to think up. It made everything meaningless.

Several minutes passed before the boy noticed that a few words had miraculously escaped. They had formed part of the story about taking a schoolgirl out to eat. This had been a late addition to the collection, and so the writer had been forced to fit his story into the space left empty by those who had come before him. As a result, four of the lines had been pushed so far to the right that the final word had spilt over on to the door-frame and thus escaped the solvent. Steve read the words over and over, trying to remember how they had fitted into the rest of the story, and exactly what it had been about. But it was no good. He hadn't even understood it at the time.

His plans to write about Tracy were forgotten. That expanse of blank wall terrified him. He had hoped to scribble a few words of homage that would have been lost among all the other stories, but to start again from scratch, to found a new tradition for others to follow, that was beyond him. Nevertheless, there was something that he *could* do. He snatched up the orange sling full of groceries and hurried back outside. Half-way down the street he stopped by a lamp-post with a bulbous base. He uncapped the pen and wrote the word EAT. After a quick glance to make sure no one had seen, he added SHIT underneath, as it had appeared on the door frame, then DIE and BOX. He put his pen away and surveyed his work with a satisfied smile. This was just the beginning. Those four poor orphaned words would come back to haunt the dark powers that had ordered and executed the destruction of the rest. They would appear everywhere, on doors and walls and public places all over the city, until no one could do anything or go anywhere without seeing them!

Steve approached the house with particular caution that day. The old man had made it clear the week before that today he would finish his long story, and the boy was worried that Hazchem might try and intervene to stop this happening. The fact that he didn't believe in the story made no difference. The old man's fear was real enough, and until that was explained it was only sensible for Steve to be frightened too.

'Now then, lad, let's see if you're still as clever at remembering what I told you.'

They had finished their tea and eggs and buttered bread, and Ernest Matthews had settled in his armchair to load and light his pipe. Steve duly recited the story of the moonlit vigil on the roof of the Hall, the footprints in the dew, Maurice's disappearance and the discovery of his body in the wood.

'Very good!' Matthews nodded. 'But I wonder if you're clever enough to guess what I thought when I heard all this, hundreds of miles away in a foreign land, on the eve of the great battle that was to be my baptism of fire? First of all, though, let me tell you exactly what it was that I heard. When Maurice's body was discovered, the police were informed and a doctor fetched to examine the corpse. He reported that death had occurred about two years before, as the result of a fall. The police immediately rounded up the forest dwellers I told you about earlier, and sure enough, they admitted burying Maurice's body. They said they had come upon it by chance one morning, and knowing that they would be turned out and made homeless a second time if it should be found there, they had dragged the body into the wood and concealed it where it might have remained undiscovered for ever if the trees had not been felled and the ground ploughed up once the war came. This much they confessed, but nothing would make them admit to the murder itself, and since there was no further evidence against them, the case remained a mystery. For my part, I was thinking of what the surgeon had said about the time of Maurice's death. It had been almost exactly two years earlier that I had watched Maurice leave the Hall one night in pursuit of a female will-o'-the-wisp. Now, there had been two sets of tracks leading away from the Hall, remember. My idea at the time had been that Maurice had gone out and then returned, but supposing he hadn't, what then?'

Steve raised his eyes to the old man's face.

'Someone followed him.'

'Good. But who?'

'His brother.'

The old man gaped.

'How . . . how did you know?'

Steve shrugged. The videos that the stotters hired often had a story of this kind as a pretext for the scenes of mayhem and carnage, and having seen a lot of them by now Steve had got quite sharp at spotting the clues.

'You said the footprints split up,' he explained. 'One lot came from the front door and the other . . . '

'From the east wing, yes. And that should have told me that they couldn't have been made by Maurice returning to the house, because all the doors save the one he'd come out of would have been bolted on the inside.'

'And his brother slept there, didn't he? And he hated him and everything.'

The old man nodded curtly. He seemed rather put out at having his thunder stolen.

'Quite so. But the question was, what was I to do? I thought of telling one of the officers, but how could I explain it all to a stranger, who didn't know the place or the people? Then I had what seemed at the time like a stroke of luck. As I said, fresh troops were constantly arriving in preparation for the attack, and one day as I was returning from fatigue duty I happened to see Maurice's friend Aubrey Deville in a lieutenant's uniform. Taking my courage in both hands, I approached him and explained the situation. It seemed a great presumption for a lad of my age, a housekeeper's son and a raw recruit, to presume to interfere in such matters. I didn't blab out my suspicions of Rupert, of course. I merely told him what I had seen that night, saying that since the discovery of Maurice's body I felt I could no longer keep silent. At first Deville listened with a condescending sort of smile, but as I spoke this slowly faded and his eyes began to probe away at me like a surgeon searching a wound. When I'd done, he stood there as silent as a statue for what seemed like an eternity. Then he nodded curtly and told me to report that afternoon to an old farm behind the lines that served as a junior officers' mess for that sector. The afternoon was a quiet time for us, when we tried to get some sleep, for we were up all night on fatigues, digging huge pits. But orders were orders, so rather regretting my rashness already I duly went to the farm, where I found Deville and a group of other officers sitting around on old ammunition boxes. My heart almost failed me when I recognized Rupert Jeffries among them. But military discipline has the great advantage that no one expects you to act naturally. I marched forward and came stiffly to attention with no more expression than a pillar-box. Aubrey Deville told me to stand at ease. "Now I want you to tell us all what you told me this morning," he says. So I did. When I had finished, Deville turned to the others and said, "You have heard this lad's evidence. I can vouch that it is true. But I can do no more than that. I can tell you what happened afterwards, and I can reveal how Maurice came by his death."

'Naturally this caused quite a stir. "When Maurice told me that he had seen this woman," Deville went on, "my first thoughts were of grave disquiet for my friend's health. All of you here knew him to some extent, but few perhaps appreciated the extent to which the catastrophe which has now overwhelmed us preyed upon his mind in those months. Maurice was increasingly distressed by the prospect of a war which he considered would plunge society into a new Dark Age, so much the more terrible than the first as our capacity for organized inhumanity is greater. In those final months of seclusion in the country, this idea had come to preoccupy him to an extent which alarmed even those of us who shared his concern. Thus when he told me about this woman who had supposedly come wandering across his lawn at midnight dressed in a shift, I feared the worst. If I agreed to sit up and watch with him, it was not in any hope that any woman would actually appear, but merely from a desire to verify my fears with a view to urging Maurice to consult a specialist in nervous diseases. But although the spirit was willing enough, the flesh proved too weak, and after waiting in vain for many weary hours, spent listening to Maurice's increasingly incoherent eulogies of this woman he claimed to have loved all his life, despite telling me he had seen her for the first time a few weeks before, I retired to get some sleep, having begged my friend to do likewise. Scarcely had I reached my room, however, than I heard Maurice's voice calling out, "Who are you? Where are you going?" The room I had been allocated was in the east wing, so I could see his window from mine, and when I looked out I beheld him gesturing frantically towards the lawn. As young Matthews here has testified, there was absolutely nothing to be seen. Maurice had already told me that he intended to follow the woman if she should appear again, so when he abruptly vanished from the window I knew what to expect. I felt that he should not be allowed to roam about all alone in the middle of the night, brainsick as I now knew him to be. Quickly drawing on again the boots I had just that moment put off, I hastened downstairs and let myself out of a side door.

'"Despite my haste, Maurice was already out of sight when I left the Hall, but the line of footprints marked in the dew on the lawn showed me the way he had gone. I followed it to the gravel path which leads from the other wing past the church to the west gate of the park. It was a fine night and I had no difficulty in finding my way. However, when I came to the gate I was at a loss. I knew that Maurice could not have gone out towards the village without rousing the gatekeeper, of whom there was no sign, but he might either have turned right towards the stables or left along the old track leading up into the woods. Then, looking in the latter direction, I seemed to see a flurry of movement about half-way up the hillside. The next moment it was gone, swallowed up in the darkness of the trees, but I immediately started running that way as fast as I could. The track was straight and steep, treacherous and uneven, the mere memory of a road. At that hour, by that light, it looked inconceivably ancient, as indeed it may well have been. The woods seemed to lower above me like a bank of fog. Once I entered their vast penumbra I could see only fitfully, by snatches. Gradually the track levelled out, and I knew that I must have reached the crest of the hill. The night was perfectly calm and still except for the sounds of my own progress and the small noises of creatures going about their business, killing and being killed. I could see almost nothing but the parting of the trees against the hazy sky, which showed me my way. At length this strip of sky broadened out as the trees on either side fell back. I thought at first that I had reached the other side of the wood, but then I saw that it was only a clearing, although a large one. In it stood a house, separated from the track by a garden with a low wall. The garden looked as wild and overgrown as the underwood itself, but the house was surprisingly handsome and large, much too imposing for a woodsman's dwelling. It may have been a hunting lodge dating from the time when those woods were a royal demesne. However that may have been, it was now quite clearly untenanted and in a state of abandonment. I was about to pass on when a jarring noise startled me. After the gentle forest murmurs I had grown used to, it sounded as loud as a shot, but I soon saw that it had been made by someone opening a window high up in one of the gables of the house. The next moment Maurice appeared at the window, smiling and waving. Overcome with relief, I hailed him. He took not the slightest notice of me, however, but continued gesturing and smiling as before. My relief rapidly turned to alarm as I realized that these demonstrations were not intended for me. 'Yes, yes!' he cried loudly. Then, to my utter horror, I beheld my friend step out and stand on the ledge. I shouted at him repeatedly, endeavouring to awaken him from his fatal delirium, but he was no more aware of me than a lover alone with his mistress is aware of the barking of a distant dog. His face was pale, rapt and ecstatic in the moonlight, even at the moment when he stepped forward off the ledge. A moment later I heard the terrible impact, like a sack hitting the ground. I rushed forward and found my friend lying on the stones of the yard. His face was uninjured, and on his lips the blissful smile I had seen before was just beginning to fade. A moment later it had gone, and his features started to set in the calm mask of death. But I had no doubt then and I have no doubt now that Maurice Jeffries died a happy man.

' "For some reason that conviction served only to increase my mortal terror of the place where I had witnessed these uncanny events. I took to my heels and ran back the way I had come as fast as I could, intending to raise the alarm. But once I was out of the wood and back in the civilized precincts of the Hall, I began to realize how incredible my story would sound. Of course, I was not to know that I had a witness in young Matthews. On the contrary, Maurice had impressed on me that he had told no one else about the woman. Surely if I were to offer such a tale, at five o'clock in the morning, as an explanation for a man's violent death, I would come under the gravest suspicion myself. After some reflection, therefore, I determined to wait until it was light, then ride out to the house in the wood as if for exercise and report the discovery of Maurice's body as though I had come upon it for the first time. It was not only to spare myself that I took this decision, but also to protect the Jeffries family from the pain and embarrassment of having to confront fully the fact that Maurice had done away with himself in a fit of madness. Perhaps I was wrong. Had I been sitting quietly in my study all evening, deliberating the issue judiciously, I might have acted otherwise. But after the horrific experience that I had just lived through, I was not quite myself. And all would have been well enough, except that when I returned to the clearing the next morning, Maurice's body was not there.

' "I was absolutely astounded. I searched the house and the garden without finding anything. In the end I began to wonder if I could have imagined the whole thing. Had it been nothing but an unusually vivid dream brought on by my wakeful night and Maurice's story? In any event, the arguments that had induced me to remain silent the night before now applied with redoubled force. In the absence of the corpse, I was left with nothing but a tissue of wild improbabilities which I had no hope of bringing anyone else to believe, since I could scarcely believe them myself. No doubt if hostilities had not broken out immediately afterwards, I would have told someone sooner or later. As it was, the matter rested there until I heard that Maurice's body had been found. But I was still at a loss what to do until Private Matthews approached me this morning. Here was a witness who would support at least half my story. I resolved to risk the rest and break my silence." '

The old man broke off suddenly, his jaws working away as though he was chewing. His breath came in little puffs through his nose. It reminded Steve of the way the stotters acted when they overdid the glue, and it suddenly occurred to the boy how easy it would be for Matthews just to keel over and never get up again. It would seem natural. The stotters had to work hard to damage themselves that badly, but the old man was like a wasp in October: bumbling, vulnerable and doomed.

'That was as much as I heard about the matter,' Matthews went on at last, 'for the next morning, just after dawn, the great attack began. It was a beautiful summer day. The sun was shining, and when our guns finally fell silent you could hear the birds singing. Then the officers blew their whistles and off we went. I wasn't afraid. We'd been told that the enemy had all been killed by our bombardment. My chief concern was to act the part and not disgrace the uniform I had tricked my way into. I tried hard not to fall like a lot of the others. We were all carrying heavy packs and I supposed they must have lost their footing somehow, but I remember saying to myself, "Here I am, a mere boy, and if I can carry on then *you* should be able to!" Then I felt something pluck my arm. It might have been someone tugging at my sleeve to attract my attention, except there was no one near. The next moment I tripped over someone lying on the ground and fell headlong like the rest. When I started to get up, I saw to my surprise that there was no one left on his feet, although just a moment before there'd been hundreds and hundreds of us walking up the hillside. I thought that there might have been an order that I hadn't heard. "Do what the others are doing" was the general rule of Army life, I'd learned, so I decided to stay where I was. My arm ached, and when I rubbed the place my hand came away all red and sticky, as if I'd been eating blackberries. I realized then that I'd been hit. It didn't bother me much at the time. I'd seen worse at home, like that time the miller's son got his leg caught under a millstone they were changing. What I didn't understand, though, was where the bullet had come from, if the enemy were all dead. I thought perhaps I'd caught one of ours going the wrong way. I could hear all manner of yelps and groans around me, mixed in with the twittering of a lark overhead. I thought I could hear a woodpecker too, and that was strange, for there were no trees near.

'The slope we were lying on, smooth and bare, reminded me of the hillside above the village. The sun grew hotter and hotter. I couldn't understand why we had been ordered to lie down, and after a while I called to the man I'd tripped over and asked him what was going on. I got no answer, so I crawled over to him. The dust all around started kicking up, the way it does when the first big raindrops hit during a summer storm. That was another strange thing, for there wasn't a cloud in the sky. When I got close enough, I saw why the man had taken no notice of me. Young as I was, I'd seen dead men before, and I knew he was dead. Then another man nearby started to lift himself up on his arms, making a kind of noise that made me look at him. I hailed him, but then the woodpecker sound started up again, and all of a sudden the man's face just disappeared, the way your reflection does if you drop a stone in a pond. It was then that I finally twigged what had happened. The enemy hadn't all been killed. They were sitting pretty in their trenches, and as we advanced they'd opened fire with machine-guns and cut us down. And the men lying on the ground around me weren't obeying some orders I hadn't heard. They were wounded or dying or dead.

'By now the sun was scorching, and when I tried to reach the water bottle in my pack I got hit again. What was making the dust kick up, I learned, was bullets. The enemy had snipers on the lookout for any movement and one of them got me through the foot. After that I could do nothing but lie still, or as still as I could with the pain, pretending to be dead. Later on, great clouds of smoke came billowing across from our side, and I saw men running forward inside it. Another attack had started, and I hoped for a moment to be rescued. But straight away that damned tap-tap-tapping started up again, and when I looked again the men were gone. After that the enemy laid down a barrage into no-man's-land, where I was. Shrapnel started flying all around, along with other things. I saw what I thought was a glove bounce on the ground just in front of me, and when I looked again I saw that it was a man's hand cut off at the wrist. When it finally started to get dark, I set off to try and crawl back to our lines. At first I tried to avoid the bodies that were lying everywhere, but in the end I just dragged myself over them, planting my hands on their stomachs and my feet in their faces. They weren't all dead, either. Many moaned and moved when I touched them, and one even begged me to shoot him, just like a child pleading for a sweet. It came on to rain, which made everything slimy and the going even more difficult. As day broke, I realized that I was still a long way from safety.

'There was a large shell-hole nearby, so I crawled in there so as to be safe from the sniper fire. My water was all gone and I had a raging thirst, so I was glad to see that a puddle of rainwater had formed at the bottom of the hole. I was about to drink when I noticed what I thought for a moment was my own reflection looking back at me. It was a corpse. He must have crawled into the hole for shelter the previous day and then drowned when the rain came on. I sat there all that day, alone in the shell-hole, staring at that dead man guarding the water that he didn't need and I couldn't drink, and listening to the shells exploding all around. I asked myself why he had died and I was still alive. There seemed to be no reason to it. Every time a shell went off, the water rippled, blurring his features. I expected to be blown to shreds every moment, or cut apart by shrapnel. But it didn't happen, and when night fell I tried once more to make my way back to our lines. By then I was almost mad with thirst, and I must have gone badly astray, for the next morning I found myself lying out in the open less than fifty yards from the enemy trenches. I could hear them calling to each other in their foreign lingo. Once in a while they loosed off a few shots when they thought they saw movement. They'd shoot at the corpses too, just for fun. The dead had begun to swell up and change colour by now, and I was afraid that the enemy would know I was alive by that. To keep my mind steady, I concentrated on watching this scrap of khaki cloth I could see, snagged on the barbed wire. It must have been part of the uniform of one of our lads who'd made it that far. All day long I watched it flapping about in the wind like some bird caught in a snare and struggling to free itself. As soon as it grew dark I set off again. Luckily it was a clear night this time, and by keeping an eye on the stars I was able to keep moving towards our lines. At daybreak I saw figures moving nearby. I didn't know if they were living creatures or ghosts, still less whether they were from our side, but I called out as loudly as I could and they came running. It was a British stretcher-party on the lookout for casualties from the previous day's action.'

The old man picked up the brass-handled poker, opened the stove and stirred the coals for some time. Steve glanced surreptitiously at the clock, which showed ten to six.

'Well, we'd better finish,' the old man sighed at last. 'There's not much left to tell, though it's the hardest part. The stretcher-bearers set me down among the other dead and wounded, and I was so exhausted that I fell asleep, lying there on the duck-boards. That was nearly the end of me, for I woke with my face underwater and such a weight on my back that I thought for a moment I must drown like a rat in our own trenches. But somehow I managed to twist myself free. A pile of the dead had fallen on top of me, as though they resented me outliving them. Later on, when I was carried back through the trench system to the rear, I saw what became of the corpses, and then I understood why we'd been set to dig those great pits before the battle. The officers had told us that the enemy would all be dead and we could just stroll across to their lines. I realized now that that was just a story, or why dig mass graves in readiness? After that I was moved from one dressing station and casualty station to another. What kept me going, despite the pain of my wounds, was the thought that now I'd be sent back home to England, having done my duty. But I was wrong. It seemed that I'd got off too lightly. To get a ticket home you needed to be more badly hurt. As soon as I was up and about again, I received orders to rejoin my unit, or rather a unit with the same name and number, for the one I'd served with had been wiped out almost to a man. The new troops were all fresh recruits who avoided me as though I had some disease. They knew well enough what had happened to us, although the officers tried to keep it secret. Twenty thousand men killed in a single day, and twice that number left mangled for life. We'd gone innocent to the slaughter, but these men knew what awaited them. I was a living reminder of that, and they wanted nothing to do with me. At that particular moment there was a lull in the fighting, so I had a lot of time to myself. My thoughts turned increasingly to home. How safe and tranquil it all seemed! I thought for the first time that I'd been happy there. I often used to think about the night I'd watched from the roof of the Hall, moving through the moonlit landscape in my thoughts. I realized that I'd been seeing it all for the last time, and that was why I'd felt so sad, because it was a leave-taking. That led me on to think about Maurice's death, and the story Aubrey Deville had told about this. And suddenly, in a flash, I saw the truth!'

He glared fiercely, challengingly, at the boy.

'Now then, you're very clever, but I wonder if you're clever enough to guess what the clue was that everyone had missed all along until I stumbled on it? A clue so blatant and obvious it was staring us all in the face all the time and yet we ignored it? Can you, eh?'

Steve shook his head. He hadn't been expecting this. The old man grinned from ear to ear with satisfaction.

'His name!' he crowed. 'Aubrey Deville. *Deville!* Take away the last two letters and what does it spell?'

The clock whirred like a slow-flying insect and struck six times.

'D,E,V,I,L!' the old man shouted. 'It was *he* who lured Maurice Jeffries to his death that night, by means of black magic! And when he followed him to the trysting-house, it was not to try and save Maurice from his fate. On the contrary, he went to gloat over his creature's act of self-destruction! Don't you see!'

Steve nodded without conviction. It sounded like the old man had been watching that video where women are walking down a street at night and these two yellow eyes glow at them out of the darkness and they burst into flame, all their clothes burning off first so you can get a good look before the skin starts crisping up. 'Pass the ketchup, darling!' Dave had yelled gleefully. And in the end it was this man they knew, only he was really the devil, and the women had it coming to them because they were nothing but slags. Steve wondered where the old man kept his video player and TV. Upstairs, perhaps. There might be all sorts of things hidden upstairs.

'About a week later,' Matthews went on, 'I was on lookout duty when I saw a figure walking towards me along the trench. I was surprised at this, for in that direction the trench ran out into no-man's-land and had been abandoned. The man didn't respond to my challenge, so I unhooded my lantern and shone it in his face. To my horror, I saw that it was none other than Deville himself, who I'd supposed was dead. He did not speak or return my salute, but simply walked past me along the trench without a glance. As soon as our watch was relieved, I told the others what had happened. The man who held the position next to mine gave me a curious look. "You must be mistaken," he said. "No one passed by me." The sergeant got to hear about this, and next day I was called to the lieutenant's quarters. "I have had inquiries made," he told me. "Lieutenant Aubrey Deville of the 8th Lincolns was killed in action over a month ago, the same day that you received your wound." He went on to caution me strongly against saying anything else that might disturb the other men or I would find myself in serious trouble. That was all very well, but two nights later the figure appeared again. At first I could make out nothing but the bulk of it, darker than the night itself, it seemed. When I shone my lantern on it and saw who it was, I guessed that Deville had come back to haunt me and lure me to my death as he had poor Maurice. I fired a shot into the air to raise the alarm, but when the others came running the figure had vanished and my story was coldly received. The next morning I was sent to see the medical officer. He said I was suffering from shell-shock and should be excused lookout duty, but the lieutenant was having none of that. "Every man under my command has to pull his weight," says he. "I've no time for malingering." That was the cruellest cut of all! No one believed me, just as no one had believed Maurice Jeffries. They all thought I was pretending to have gone off my head so as to get sent home. After that all was quiet again for several nights. This is the way he likes to strike, coming on you when you least expect it. Then one day news came that a fresh attack was being planned for the following morning. We spent the night in the front-line trenches. About three in the morning Deville appeared again. He came straight at me this time, those eyes of his looking through me and an evil grin on his lips. I seized my rifle and warned him off, and when he took no notice I fired. As ill luck would have it, the shot struck one of the other men in the trench. He wasn't badly hurt, but not even the lieutenant wanted me around after that, of course. I was packed off back to England, where they shut me up in a hospital for mental cases in a big house in the country. It was not so very different from the Hall, and the remarkable thing was that from the moment I entered that place Deville never troubled me again. Not that it was a holiday in other respects! They treated us cruelly, burning us with electric current and cigarettes. It was like medicine, they said, to shock us out of our shock, but I reckoned it was a test, to see who wanted bad enough to stay. Well, I did, for I knew I was safe from Deville as long as I stayed there.

'At long last the fighting stopped. Shortly afterwards, my mother was carried off by the influenza that came along to sweep up the war's leavings. I was let out of hospital to attend the funeral, and I had half a mind to slip away afterwards. But just as they were lowering the coffin into the ground, I looked up and there he stood, as plain as anything, on the other side of that awful pit, grinning at me. I pointed him out to the others, calling him a murderer to his face. But of course they thought I was having one of my fits again, and packed me off back to the hospital. I went gladly enough, for my dreams of freedom had all turned sour. I knew that I would never be safe from him anywhere but in the hospital. Remember that, lad, if ever you have need. Get into hospital, whatever it costs you, for there and only there will you be safe from him. I would still be there myself if they hadn't put me out in the end. There was another war coming by then, and they needed the space I dare say. Luckily for me, I had a place to go. When my mother left service, she had gone to live with her maiden sister in this very house, and when the sister died in her turn she willed me the house and everything in it, having no family herself. I've lived here ever since, never seeing anyone nor hardly setting foot outside the door. For if ever I do step out, he's sure to be lying in wait for me.'

A silence fell. The old man looked at the boy and shrugged. He looked dull and diminished. Steve stood up, taking his orange sling.

'I got to be going.'

'Will you come again, now you know the danger?' Matthews asked him anxiously.

'What you mean?'

'Why, you've seen him yourself! You said you saw him watching the house, following you home. If he knows you're helping me then he'll try and destroy you too.'

Steve shook his head awkwardly.

'It isn't the same person.'

Matthews snorted indignantly.

'How do you know?'

'All those blokes, they were older than you, right? The one I seen is only about twenty, twenty-five.'

The old man stared at the boy in silence.

'Why, you don't think he's *alive*, do you?' he exclaimed.

ELEVEN

Steve walked home slowly, pushing against a strengthening wind which was breaking up the cloud cover. Well, he would have told it differently, that was all he could say. He'd have had hidden treasure, a big chest stuffed with gold and jewels which the old man had taken from the place in the country after the brothers got killed and kept in a room somewhere at the top of the house, where no one ever went. Hazchem would have been the son of Maurice and the woman on the lawn, so the treasure belonged to him, or at least he reckoned it did, which was why he kept watching Matthews's house. That sounded much more likely than all the stuff about ghosts and devils. The boy's doubts about Ernest Matthews had been proved too right. Houses under the sea and rich people living in cemeteries had turned out to be the least of it, in the end. Matthews's fear itself was fake. The danger and mystery which had haunted these streets for weeks, lending drama to Steve's life, stood revealed as nothing more than the pathetic delusions of an old man who'd lost his mind somewhere along the way.

Even decorating a garage door and a pillar-box with EAT SHIT DIE BOX didn't help. It wasn't until Steve reached Trencham Road that he forgot all about his disappointment and the old man. It was at once obvious that something out of the ordinary had happened: the corrugated iron fence that surrounded the house had been torn down and the garden churned into a slurry of mud in the midst of which lay piles of wooden hoarding and bundles of barbed wire. At the side of the house nearest the corner stood a large skip covered with a tarpaulin, and a yellow bulldozer. There was no one about. Whoever had done all this had gone away again, for the moment. The boy walked round the corner, then doubled back across the end of the ruined wilderness, thankful that it was starting to get dark by now. He paused in a patch of undergrowth which the bulldozer had missed, crouching down and sniffing the dense rank odour of the nettles, listening intently. All was quiet. He scurried over the open ground, skidding on the slippery gashes of bare clay, to the back door. He wriggled past the plywood screen, inside the house.

The passageway was dark, but a glow up ahead showed that a light was on in the living room. The boy picked his way along the exposed floor joists and odd patches of floorboard that hadn't gone into the fire. Dave's ravages had left a gap of almost a yard between a joist at the door and the beginning of the flooring, making it impossible to come into the room gradually. Steve stood there for several minutes, craning his neck and trying to make sense of the faint noises he could hear. It was a mumbling sound, rather like a baby. In the end he took a deep breath and jumped.

On one of the mattresses lay Tracy, the earphones of the Walkman almost lost in her hair. She was wearing a pink skirt over black tights and a white T-shirt printed with a cartoon of a leering orange cat and the words 'Stick with me, kid – we'll go places'. A bottle of Drambuie was balanced on her stomach, rising and falling with each breath she took. Her little feet twitched in time to the inaudible music and she was half-singing the words. She waved to Steve and pulled the earphones off.

'Here, have a listen.'

He knelt down and took the flimsy hoop, still warm from the girl's head. Tracy raised the bottle of Drambuie to her mouth. A bubble of air slipped between her lips and the glass rim and rose slowly through the dense brown liquid. She held the bottle out to Steve. The boy shook his head.

'Go on! You got to start sometime.'

He took the bottle and their fingers touched for a moment. He tilted it to his mouth, as she had done. The rim was wet, and when the liqueur trickled down his throat, sweet and hot and perfumed, he imagined that he was tasting her saliva. Her body was terrifyingly close to his. All he had to do was reach out and touch her.

'Where are the others?' he asked, handing back the bottle.

'Out looking for a place to stay. Can't stop here now, can we?'

Tracy's was not a successful face, which was one reason why Steve liked it. Some faces were like television; there was nothing to do except sit and look at them. But Tracy's was a d-i-y face. You needed to spend time on it, but it gave you a great sense of satisfaction and achievement. Without make-up, her features looked as raw, vulnerable and unglamorous to Steve as his own. He had never looked at her from so close before. He knew at once that it would be useless to try to hide anything from her. This came as a great relief.

Tracy pressed a button on the Walkman and music abruptly exploded inside Steve's head. He watched as she started packing her clothes into crumpled plastic bags. The music made her every gesture seem special and significant, like a film. When the song was over, Steve took the earphones off.

'When we leaving?' he asked.

'Later on. This place'll be gone tomorrow. Funny, isn't it?'

Although she was only a few yards away, Steve had the feeling that they were separated by an enormous distance.

'Can I have a bit more of that stuff?' he asked, to bring her back.

Tracy turned to him, grinning.

'Can't get enough once you get started, can you?'

She came and knelt beside him and they both drank. When Tracy started to get up again, she lost her balance and reached for the boy's shoulder to steady herself. That pushed him over too, and they fell over together on the mattress. The next moment something wet and warm happened to Steve's face. By the time he realized that Tracy was kissing him, she had finished. She leaned back, staring up at the ceiling. Her face was still only inches from his, yet this distance seemed even more achingly unbridgeable than the one which had separated them earlier. Miniature music leaked from the earphones abandoned on the mattress beside them, mixed in with the hollow booming of the wind in the chimney. Tracy's hair had started to grow out from the roots again in its natural mousy colour, as though the spell that had temporarily transformed her into a glamorous witch was slowly wearing off.

'So anyway, what's this you've been getting up to?' she asked.

'How do you mean?'

'Shopping for some old fucker and that.'

She groped for the bottle and had another swig.

'Well, he can't get out of the house,' Steve explained.

'What, crippled, is he?'

Steve shook his head, then tapped it with two fingers. 'Bit mental. He lives in this big house, in this one room downstairs, all full of stuff. But he won't go outside, see? Thinks somebody's going to do him.'

'Fuck.'

Tracy sounded impressed.

'He won't even open the door, only to me,' Steve bragged. 'I got to ring the bell in a special way, otherwise he won't come.'

'How do you mean, special?'

'Like this.'

He tapped out the rhythm on the floor. Tracy yawned.

'Sounds a right loony.'

She lay staring up at the ceiling for a while. Then she rolled up and leaned over the boy, flicking her tongue around the whorls of his ear. Steve started and quivered in her grasp, moaning with surprise and pleasure. His throat was dry and his heart pounding. He wished that this had never started, and that it would never end. He twisted round to face her, reached out and placed his hands on her ribs. He could feel the underside of her breasts pressing against the base of his thumbs. This was just as he had imagined it in the stories he used to tell himself: the stotters gone, Tracy come to him, the warmth and the cuddles. Was it possible to make things happen by imagining them, by telling stories about them?

'So where does he keep it all?' Tracy asked, putting the earphones back on her head and adjusting the volume. Steve blinked at her.

'What?'

There was a long pause before she answered.

'The money he gives you for the shopping and that. If he don't ever go out, he must have it stashed away somewhere.'

Steve felt it would be a shame to ruin the good impression he seemed to be making by admitting that he didn't know the answer to this question.

'It's in this big trunk upstairs,' he said, remembering his improved version of the old man's story.

'Get out,' Tracy murmured.

Oddly enough, the fact that Steve knew his story wasn't true only increased his resentment at not being believed.

'It is! I've been up there! I've seen it! There's this old trunk full of gold and jewels and stuff, in a big room up at the top of the house.'

Tracy said nothing. Her eyes were closed and her body twitched in time to a music only she could hear. Steve assumed that she had already forgotten what they had been talking about. He had grown used to the fact that the stotters' attention span lasted only a few moments.

'Where the fuck those wankers got to?' she remarked at last, turning off the Walkman. 'We got to get out of here, find somewhere to live! They'll pull this place down around us if we stay.'

Mistaking this for a joke, Steve laughed. Tracy twisted indignantly out of his grasp and sat up.

'They fucking *will*!' she shouted. 'Bastards, that's all they are! Fucking bastards.'

Steve felt as though half his body had been torn away. He had lost her. But how could he have guessed that she would still be worrying about things like that after what had just happened? Couldn't she feel the amazing power generated by their closeness, the energy that set the air between them humming and crackling like high-voltage electricity? This stuff too, he sensed, could light and heat your life, and kill you.

'Here, what about this old geezer?' Tracy demanded suddenly. 'We could stay there! Where's he live?'

Steve didn't know what to say. What she was suggesting was unthinkable, of course, out of the question. But how could he explain that?

'Where's he live?' Tracy repeated urgently.

Steve shrugged.

'Long way off.'

'Where?'

'Other side of the main road.'

'By the Esso?'

'Other way.'

'What, by Tesco's?'

'You know the park? Round there.'

'That's where Debbie lives!' the girl exclaimed triumphantly. 'She'd be just round the corner.'

'Who's Debbie?'

'Paxton Grove, that's where Debbie lives, her and the baby. It's all council, most of it. Is that it?'

'Sort of.'

'What do you mean, sort of? Don't you even know the name of the street?'

'It's on the corner, isn't it?' Steve replied with a touch of irritation.

'Which corner? By the park?'

'No, the other end. Grafton Avenue. But look, it's no good. He won't let us in.'

'If you ring that special way . . .'

'He's frightened of strangers – '

'We're *not* strangers!' Tracy shouted angrily. 'We're friends, aren't we? Friends of yours.'

Steve fell silent. He just couldn't get across to her the impossibility of what she was proposing. Tracy had another drink and offered him the bottle, but Steve shook his head, which felt quite muddled enough already. The girl thrust the bottle in his face.

'Go on!'

It was more a threat than an offer. Steve raised the bottle to his lips, but kept them closed to prevent any of the liquid entering his mouth. Tracy snuggled down beside him, her left hand ruffling his hair. Steve lay there as stiff as a corpse. Something that could only be the girl's other hand was prowling about on his jeans, smoothing and squeezing the material over his penis.

'*We* could just go,' she murmured in his ear. 'You and me. He wouldn't be frightened of me, would he? Not of a girl.'

For the first time, Steve began to think that maybe there was some point to what the stotters got up to in the evening. If it felt anything like this, that would explain a lot, even the stories in the lavatory. He had often done it to himself, of course, what Tracy was doing to him, but he'd never realized the difference when someone else did it to you. He wondered what he could do to her in return, to make her feel what he was feeling.

'What number is it?'

Her voice seemed to come from very far away. Steve had no idea what she was talking about.

'The house,' she prompted.

'Number two.'

He was going on to explain that it wouldn't work, not even just the two of them, because old Matthews was so far gone that he was quite capable of thinking that Tracy was the devil in drag. But there was no one to explain to, for the girl had taken her hand away, got up and walked out of the room. The floor seemed to be shaking beneath him, as though the wind was making the whole house shudder. It made him feel slightly sick. It was the booze, of course. He was just drunk, fucked up, out of it. He couldn't understand where Tracy had gone so suddenly, unless she'd had to pee. He lay there, waiting patiently for her to come back.

But she didn't. Instead, wee Alex appeared in the doorway.

'Come on,' he said.

As the epithet that invariably accompanied his name suggested, Alex looked as though he'd been conceived on the cheap. There was a low-budget, no frills air about him which perhaps explained why Steve had never been frightened of Alex in the way he was of Dave or Jimmy. What had happened the week before had made no difference. The boy knew that Alex had just been trying to keep in good with Dave. He would have done the same himself in the circumstances.

'Where we going?' he asked as he got to his feet.

'Ask no questions, you'll be told no lies,' Alex recited mechanically.

Steve looked round the room at the mattresses and the plastic bags full of Tracy's things.

'Shall I take something?'

Then Dave's voice, outside the room, roared, 'Just hurry the fuck up!'

Steve got moving. He had learned the hard way never to make Dave say things twice, because that wound him up. So when they got to the hallway, he was relieved to see that Dave looked quite calm. Tracy was there too, putting on her black and white make-up. Alex pointed to the stairs, wiggling his forefinger back and forth.

'Upstairs?' Steve frowned. 'Why, what's up there?'

Dave laughed.

' "What's up there?" ' he mimicked several times.

Each time the question made him laugh afresh. Alex and Tracy joined in the laughter, but Steve sensed that their hearts weren't in it. They were just trying to keep on the right side of Dave, as usual. This seemed sensible, so Steve laughed as well.

'What's so funny?' Dave demanded aggressively. There was no trace of humour in his voice or on his face. Alex punched Steve on the shoulder. The boy felt totally confused. It was as if they had all changed parts: Tracy had treated him like one of the stotters, while Alex was coming on tough like Dave. Steve couldn't think who Dave was acting like, but certainly not himself.

'Get the fuck upstairs!' Alex told him.

This was easier said than done. The lower flight had been so extensively quarried for firewood that nothing remained but the framework, like a ladder without rungs. Steve and Alex clambered up, followed more slowly by Dave. When they reached the landing, Alex pushed Steve forward into one of the two bedrooms at the rear of the property. There was no electricity upstairs, but a faint glimmer from the next street showed an extent of bare boards and peeling wallpaper. Dave inspected the lock with a look of disgust that reminded Steve of Jimmy. Was that whose part Dave had taken? But then where did that leave Jimmy?

'Might have known it,' he complained. 'No fucking key.'

Alex gave the lock a brief glance.

'If I had another of them hangers . . .'

He nodded at the cupboard built into one corner of the room.

'What's the matter?' Dave sneered. 'You scared?'

He walked over to the cupboard and disappeared inside. A moment later he reappeared holding a wire clothes-hanger. Alex straightened out the loop at the top, stuck it into the lock and twiddled it back and forth, bending it against the edge of the keyhole. The bolt emerged with a sharp click.

'Fucking brilliant,' said Dave.

He and Alex turned to go out. Steve made to go with them, but Dave pushed him back.

'Where you think you're going?'

'Thus far and no further,' Alex supplied.

Steve looked from one of them to the other in bewilderment.

'But those men, they'll be back in the morning! They'll find me here! I'll get into trouble!'

Dave shook his head.

'No, no, no, no, no,' he said firmly, pronouncing each negative with great care and weight. 'No, don't you worry about that. They won't find you, old son. They'll just tear down the whole fucking place with you inside, that's what they'll do.'

'What goes up must come down,' mused Alex.

'They'll just ram that bulldozer at the wall, again and again and again and again,' Dave went on with mounting enthusiasm, 'until the whole fucking lot comes down, hundreds and hundreds of tons of it crushing you slowly to a bleeding pulp, your eyes popping out and your balls exploding and the blood gushing out of your ears. Pity we can't be here to watch.'

Steve's dash to the door was swift and sudden, but Alex threw himself at the boy's ankles and dragged him down.

'A match-winning tackle from the man they said was over the hill,' he crowed. 'The old skills still there.'

They put the boot in a few times and then flung Steve back into the bedroom.

'Let me go!' the boy pleaded. 'Just let me run off! You won't see me no more, I promise. I won't bother you. Just don't leave me here alone!'

An internal pain seemed to wrench Dave's features out of joint. Steve was so unused to seeing any expression at all on that pallid face that it was several moments before he realized that Dave was grinning.

'But you're *not* alone!' he said.

The two stotters burst out laughing. The door slammed behind them and there was a rattling as the wire turned in the lock. Then there was silence, broken only by a murmur of voices outside the house. Steve rushed to the window, but there was nothing to be seen but the vandalized garden, bright in the moonlight. He ran back to the door and pulled and twisted and shook the handle for a uselessly long time. Would the demolition men search the house before starting work? Why would they bother? He could try screaming for help, but would they hear his cries above the roar of their machinery? If only he had a rope, he could smash the window and climb down. For a moment he thought of using electric wiring ripped from the light fixture or from under the floor. But he couldn't reach the ceiling, and the floorboards in the bedrooms were all intact, owing to the difficulty of access once Dave had shortsightedly demolished the stairs. Which left only the cupboard.

Steve's first impression on opening the door was that the confined space inside was full of clothes. Since the stotters didn't go in for extensive wardrobes, he supposed that these must have been left there by the previous occupiers. Remembering an escape film they'd watched one night, he wondered if he could rip the clothes into strips and make them into a rope. Then he noticed the shoes. They were ordinary enough, grubby blue and white trainers worn at the heel. What was unusual was that they were not resting on the floor but hovering in the air several inches above it.

By now the boy's eyes had adjusted to the darkness, and it was becoming clear that a lot of what he had taken for clothes was in fact just shadow. The cupboard actually contained only one set of garments, bulked out to look like more. It took a little longer to work out just what it was that was filling out the dirty jeans, pullover and jacket, and supporting the shoes in mid-air. The wire hanger fastened to one of the brass wall-hooks had been twisted so tightly that the chubby face had broken out in blood as though it had been skinned. Despite this, Steve had no difficulty in recognizing Jimmy.

The boy's second assault on the door left his hands ringing

like bells and his throat raw from howling out the forbidden word.

'Mum! Mum! Help! Let me out, Mum!'

He only stopped when he thought he heard the corpse coming at him from behind, the head like a boiled beetroot and the feet not touching the floor. Before he could look round and make sure, darkness took over the room, setting everything free. Steve panicked. He ran for his life, hitting the wall so hard he saw flashes inside his head. He dropped to the floor, writhing madly about in pain and despair, flailing around with his fists and kicking out with both feet, raging and screaming in the dark.

By the time the moon came out again, the boy had collapsed into a whimpering huddle. He staggered to the window and looked out. The cloud had passed, but there were others about. He strained at the casement without effect: the window was sealed shut with paint. Steve removed one of his shoes and hit the glass repeatedly until it broke and the wind poured in. He cleared away most of the fragments and leaned out. Some way below the window a waste-pipe from the bathroom ran across to the corner of the house. The moonlight made everything curiously two-dimensional and it was difficult to estimate how far below the window the pipe was. But it didn't really matter. He had to get out of the room before another cloud crossed the moon, and there was no other way.

Steve put his shoe back on again and carefully picked the remaining fragments of glass out of the frame. Then he got on to the window sill, turned over to lie on his stomach and lowered himself out until his chest was resting on the ledge outside. This was the point of no return. If he let himself go any further, he wouldn't be able to pull himself back in again. He still couldn't feel the pipe under his feet, but it couldn't be far. To clinch the matter, the boy reminded himself of what was in that room, allowing himself a mental glimpse inside the cupboard as though he were switching a torch on and off. That was enough. He let himself slip out a bit more, and then a bit more, and then he no longer had a choice. He dropped, hanging full-length from the window frame, the wind flapping his trousers. But his feet, like those of the corpse, were still swinging in mid-air.

He had another brief fit of sobbing and pleading, but it didn't last long. He had to strain for breath as it was, with his chest stretched tight by his raised arms. Besides, his fingers, already bruised from his assault on the door and now slippery with sweat as well, were gradually losing their grip on the glossy paint. He beat his feet wildly against the wall, trying vainly to find a purchase, but he soon realized how useless it was. There was nothing whatever he could do. When the moment came he was calm and still, although his eyes were screwed tightly shut so that he wouldn't have to see what was going to happen. Then his fingers let go and he fell. Almost at once he felt a steady pressure on the soles of his shoes. The waste-pipe must have been just below his feet as he hung from the window frame, and because he had not struggled he had been able to keep his balance as he dropped on to it. But he couldn't continue to do so for long. His arms, still outstretched above his head, were already shaking, and an uncontrollable trembling was breaking out all over his body. The pipe he was standing on was narrow and coated in shiny black paint that felt slippery, and it ran at quite a steep angle from the bathroom outlet to its junction with the downpipe. Gusts of wind tugged and pulled at his clothes. Then everything disappeared again as another cloud covered the moon.

Steve hugged the wall, pressing himself up against it as though it were a warm firm body, and suddenly the memory of what had happened with Tracy came back to him with triumphant force. That had *happened*, he thought. It wasn't just a story, even though it had started off as one. It was real, it was true. Nothing could alter the fact that he had held Tracy in his arms, that she had kissed him and put her tongue in his ear and he had touched her breasts. The trembling left him, as though by magic, and he was no longer bothered by the darkness. He edged his way up the pipe until he felt his hands touch the ledge outside the bathroom window. This one wouldn't budge either, so he took off his shoe again, clinging on to the ledge one-handed, then stretched as high as he could and beat the heel against the glass. It had no effect, and when the light returned he saw that the window was made of tough frosted glass. Because he was standing so close to it, he could only hit it feebly. Then a gust of wind caught him off balance and for a moment he seemed to hang in mid-air, sustained by nothing but his fear. Grabbing the ledge again, he renewed his assault on the window. By the time the glass finally cracked he was shaking uncontrollably and mouthing futile pleas. There was no question of removing all the pieces of broken glass this time. He knocked out the largest and sharpest ones, threw his shoe inside and leapt after it. His hands flailed for purchase against the sides of the frame, slashing themselves on the jagged edges. He hung there for a long time, wriggling and twisting. Gradually his spasms moved him forward over the frame until his centre of gravity was once again inside the house. After that it was just a matter of slithering head first to the floor, where he lay sobbing among the fragments of broken glass until he remembered where he was and realized that the stotters might come back if they failed to find anywhere else to spend the night. The house was dark and silent. He negotiated the stairs, pushed back the plywood screen on the back door and left.

It was a shock at first to be back in the familiar streets and find them unchanged, to see cars passing by and people walking their dogs. 'Don't you wankers understand where you are yet?' he felt like screaming at them. 'Haven't you realized that there's only one way out of this place?' But soon it was his own experience that came to seem bizarre, dubious and exaggerated. Things like that don't happen, he thought, not really. By the time he reached Paxton Grove, the whole episode had come to seem like one of the stories he made up to tell himself or other people. Then he saw Hazchem striding along the pavement towards him, his arms swinging back and forth like a mad soldier, his lips fixed in the usual rictus.

Steve stepped into the gateway of the house he was passing and looked round for cover. A car with no wheels was parked in the concreted-over front garden, its axles supported on piles of breeze-blocks, and the boy crouched down behind it. It was as well to be cautious, even though he was no longer seriously afraid of Hazchem. He knew now that the man's mocking grin expressed exactly what he himself had felt as he watched the dozy householders shuffling round the block behind their obese pampered pets. Steve had travelled a long way that evening. Hazchem must have made that journey too, only he had somehow got lost and been unable to find his way back. When he got to the house he would tell the old man all this. He would explain to him that there was really no reason to be afraid. Steve's cuts were starting to smart badly now, and he had just noticed that his clothes were heavily stained with blood. The rapid tattoo of footsteps suddenly ceased, quite close by. For a moment Steve thought that he'd been spotted and Hazchem was going to come up and ask him if he knew what time it was. Then he heard a door slam, and realized what should have been obvious to him all along. No wonder he'd seen the grinning man around there so many times! The boy straightened up, smiling to himself at the thought of what Ernest Matthews would say when he told him that the man he went in such terror of lived just round the corner, that they were practically neighbours!

The house in Grafton Avenue looked reassuringly the same as ever. Its end wall still towered blindly over the adjacent property as though disdaining to take any notice of what went on there, its deeply bayed front still sought to dominate the street with a pompous pretension that was rather pathetic. Steve pushed open the gate and followed the winding path into the lean-to porch. He didn't have the slightest doubt that the old man would take him in. He would have to. He needed him.

As he reached the top step, the boy stopped dead. The front door stood wide open and a cold draught streamed past, scattering the familiar smells that usually greeted Steve like eager pets. He stood there for a long time before realizing that further resistance was pointless. Then he let the current carry him forward the way he had to go, over the threshold, into the house.

TWELVE

'Well then, it's about bloody time you got your act together, isn't it?'

The slow rhythmic throbbing sound from next door continued. It sounded rather like someone trying to start a car with a flat battery.

'Because it's your *responsibility*, that's why,' Jenny Wilcox told the phone. 'This is a stand-up-and-be-counted situation! I'm damned if I'm having my members used as cannon fodder so that you lot can decide whether the battle's worth fighting or not.'

She slammed the receiver down. For a moment the throbbing sound seemed to have faded, then it returned, peaking and dying as though carried from a distance on gusts of wind. Brushing a few stray crumbs off her leotard, Jenny went over and opened the door to Aileen's office.

'Christ, what's wrong?'

Aileen sat slumped over her desk, head lowered, shoulders trembling. When she lifted her head, her face looked blurred and soft, like pottery which had lost its glaze and was gradually unbaking itself, returning to the damp clay.

'He waited for her to wake up,' she murmured.

'Who?'

'He just sat there beside the bed, waiting for her to wake up.'

'Who? Where? When?'

Despite Jenny's real concern, there was a note of irritation in her voice. Aileen sucked in enough air to stem her sobs and justify her emotion.

'It's Steven. I've been to the police. They told me . . .'

'The police?'

The younger woman's evident disapproval brought Aileen round like a whiff of ammonia.

'It's a police matter,' she replied flatly, scrabbling in her bag for Kleenex and cigarettes. 'They showed me the photographs. Everything thrown about, ripped up, smashed, destroyed, the old man beaten to death. Steven was covered in blood from the cuts he got escaping from the other house, so when one of the neighbours saw him leaving they phoned the police. A patrol car picked him up just a few streets away. Naturally they thought he'd done it.'

Jenny tilted her head experimentally in various directions.

'Just unblocking my synapses,' she explained. 'I got embroiled in a slanging match with the area organizer about this planned day of action. Now then, what were you saying? I don't really understand what this has to do with someone waiting for someone to wake up.'

'It's my fault, Jenny, I'm not explaining it well. I'll tell you some other time.'

'No, tell me now.'

Aileen would have much preferred not to do so, but after letting Jenny see her break down she felt a need to demonstrate control.

'All right. Well, let's begin at the beginning. The police had no difficulty in tracing Steven's background once they knew his real name. His life is exceptionally well documented, in fact. He's been in and out of one file or another since the day he was born. That happened in Holloway, where his mother was doing eighteen months for her part in a dope-smuggling operation. Once she got out of prison, things went from bad to worse. Petty theft, a bit of prostitution, then a heroin habit. She ended up in council emergency housing in a bed-and-breakfast in Bayswater. It sounds like an urban concentration camp. One room, one bed, one toilet and kitchen between thirty people.'

'I hear some councils are thinking of moving their homeless to pre-fab settlements on the outskirts of the city,' Jenny commented. 'Sort of a township concept. We've a lot to learn from the South Africans in this respect, I always say.'

'One day Steven's mother took an overdose, by accident or on purpose. The room was kept bolted from the inside, for protection. Those places are pretty rough, the police said. People get raped and beaten up on the stairs. But Steven was only seven years old. He wasn't strong enough to open the bolts by himself, even after he realized that his mother wasn't going to wake up. In the end someone heard his hammering on the door, but it took a long time. No one paid much attention to screams or banging in that place. When they broke down the door the body was starting to decompose. She'd been dead almost a week. Steven had been with her all that time, waiting for her to wake up.'

Aileen grabbed a deep breath and tried to ride the wave of emotion that threatened her. In the end it rolled by without breaking.

'I must go,' she said, glancing at her watch. 'Steven's social worker is coming to pick him up at three, and I have to try and explain things to him first. What are you doing this evening, Jenny? Douglas is away, and I was wondering if – '

'Jon and I have to go to a do at LWT, unfortunately. The usual rent-a-celebrity crowd will be there and it's important for him to get out and network-build. Did I tell you that he's in this big new series on famine they're planning? Off-camera, but you'll hear him interviewing the victims. He's quite high profile in Third World disasters, apparently.'

Catching Aileen's eye, Jenny covered herself by laughing cynically. 'We're having a few people over tomorrow for fondue bourguignonne,' she said as she turned to go. 'Drop by if you like. I expect we can find an extra fork.'

'I'm going away, actually,' Aileen lied.

She stubbed out her cigarette and walked over to the window, with floorboards flexing beneath her. The glass was flecked with drops of rain so fine they seemed to hang motionless in the air, as though the clouds had collapsed under their own weight like an old ceiling. She stood there thinking how clever she'd been, explaining away her emotion without mentioning its real cause. For Aileen hadn't told Jenny everything she'd learned from the police, not by a long chalk. She hadn't told her that one reason why Steven and his mother had been living in squalor was that the woman's lover, who was also the courier who brought the cannabis in from the Continent, had absconded with her savings, which she'd given him to buy them tickets to safety. By then she knew that she was pregnant, and she'd also begun to suspect that her house in south London, which was used to store the drugs, was under surveillance. When the police finally moved in, a few weeks later, her lover was the only one to escape arrest. Steven's mother told the police that he'd arranged to meet her at Heathrow with the tickets, but didn't turn up. It was later established that he had flown from Gatwick to Holland and then back to his native America. The case was relatively insignificant by US standards, and it hadn't been thought worthwhile to apply for extradition, even though the man's name and address were known to the police, as indeed they were to Aileen.

That explained a lot, she thought. It explained the likeness between Steven and Raymond, which had so disturbed her. It explained Raymond's frequent unexplained absences from Brighton, and the fact that he always had plenty of money even though his father proved to be neither rich nor generous. It explained why a man so attractive to women had taken up with a girl like Aileen, plain and shy but so 'typically English and straight' that her presence on the pillion of his motorbike ensured that he was always waved through Customs after their brief trips across the Channel. It explained why he had flown back to America so unexpectedly, supposedly to visit a mother who later turned out to have been dead for years, and why he hadn't bothered to answer Aileen's passionate letters or seemed particularly overjoyed when she turned up on his doorstep that summer. She should have felt relieved, she supposed. Her instincts had been justified; she wasn't crazy after all. Raymond really was the boy's father. That should have made her feel better, but it didn't. In fact she didn't feel anything very much, not yet. Her tears had been for the boy. As for herself, she was like a character in a cartoon film who has walked off the edge of a cliff without realizing it and strolls blithely on in defiance of the laws of gravity, protected by his blissful ignorance. Sooner or later, she knew, the reality of what had happened would come home to her and she would drop like a stone.

Her breath had misted the glass in front of her, obscuring the view. Idly she traced the words EAT, SHIT, DIE, BOX with her fingertip. Then she hastily rubbed them out, clearing the glass. There was work to do, and thanks to what the police had told her she was able to approach her talk with Steven in a more positive frame of mind than she would have imagined possible a few hours earlier. The information might have been personally devastating, but professionally it was a godsend. For the first time, Aileen felt that she understood the situation in depth, clearly and completely. Steven Bradley had already suffered more than enough pain for one lifetime, but from now on, she vowed, things would be different. His mother and father were both dead, but the boy would be saved from the wreckage to grow up whole and healthy. Everyone who had come into contact with him agreed that the core of his personality was still intact; indeed, this was one reason why he had not been considered ill enough to warrant in-patient status. But the proper treatment of his psychological injuries had been hampered by their ignorance of their real cause and nature. Now that had been cleared up, Aileen felt confident that he would make a swift and full recovery.

She timed her arrival in Green Ward for just before two o'clock, so as to catch the boy before he could go off with the others to start the afternoon's activities. When she entered the ward sitting room, Steven was gamely trying to clean the floor with a large industrial vacuum cleaner which made so much noise that he didn't hear her call him. Aileen stood watching with the feeling of slight distaste that always came over when she saw patients performing tasks labelled 'work therapy', although in her view this amounted to little more than coping with staff shortages by exploiting the patients in a way that confirmed their tendency to become institutionalized. It was only after some time that she realized that these thoughts were only possible because the giddy sense of vertigo that had always threatened her encounters with the boy was completely absent. Now she knew the source of those mysterious promptings, their power had been exorcized. When Steven finally switched off the vacuum cleaner, it cost Aileen no effort to go up to him, touch him gently on the shoulder and say, in a kindly but restrained tone, 'Steven, I'd like a word with you, please.'

They sat down together on a sofa facing the outer wall, whose chessboard pattern here generated two large windows at knee level and half of another just below the ceiling.

'Did you enjoy your lunch?' Aileen asked while she waited for the other patients to disperse. As usual, the boy just shrugged.

'I didn't have any,' she went on. 'I didn't have time. I had to go and see the police. They're very pleased, because they've finally caught the person who did those terrible things. And it's all thanks to you, Steven.'

He glanced at her with a look of alarm.

'Me?'

Aileen nodded and gave him an approving smile.

'Once they'd learned your real name, you see, they checked their records and discovered that you'd been taken to a police station once before. The sergeant who was on duty that day remembered that two other young people had been there at the same time. One of them had claimed that you were his brother, and you'd gone away with them. Their names had been taken too. One of them was called Jimmy and the other one Dave.'

She paused for a moment, watching the boy. He was glacially still, as though in a state of suspended animation.

'Dave is now in prison. He was arrested for assaulting an old lady and taking her money. Another boy, called Alex, was arrested with him.'

The squelch of shoes came and went in the corridor. A voice called, 'How should I know where it's got to? First I heard we've even got one.' 'Didn't you read the circular?' someone yelled back.

'Dave refused to co-operate with the police, but Alex did. He said that you used to live with them in a house they were squatting in. There was a girl there as well, a girl called Tracy.'

'Did they get her too?' Steve demanded.

'Who?'

'The police!'

Aileen shook her head. The boy released a long sigh and every muscle in his body seemed to relax.

'Alex said that he and Dave saw you at the supermarket one day,' Aileen continued. 'They realized that someone was paying you to go shopping. Dave and Jimmy had started robbing old people in the street by this time, but they never got much money. Jimmy decided that the person you did the shopping for must have a lot of money hidden away somewhere to pay you with. He told the girl to try and find out from you where the house was.'

A spasm like a single shiver ran through the boy's body. Then he was absolutely still again, the pulsing of an artery on his neck the only sign that he was still alive.

'But before they could do anything, workmen arrived to demolish the house. Jimmy and Dave started to argue about what to do and how to divide up the money they thought they were going to get. Alex and Tracy went out to fetch something to drink. When they came back, Jimmy was lying on the floor. His face was all discoloured. Dave said that he'd had a heart attack. He told Alex to help him carry the body upstairs and hide it in a cupboard. When they got upstairs, Jimmy suddenly started to twitch, but Dave got a coat-hanger and twisted it around his neck. Then he and Alex hung the body up in the cupboard to hide it from the workmen.'

The Unit was swathed in mist as though in cotton wool. Normally you could hear the distant noise of traffic, but today they might have been somewhere deep in the country. Aileen's efforts to make her voice calm and soothing made her sound, to her own ears at least, like a radio programme called *Listen With Mother*. Every afternoon she and her mother had sat down in front of the wireless set and listened to a well-modulated female voice telling stories about the doings of bunnies, ducks and teddies. While she listened, Aileen had studied the lighted panel at the top of the wireless, displaying the names of foreign cities: Moscow, Rome, Warsaw, Berlin, Tokyo. The world was vast and various, fascinating but utterly safe, populated by furry little creatures who might occasionally be just a little bit naughty. No wonder people go mad, she thought.

The only point at which Steven had seemed at all disturbed by her narrative had been when she mentioned the girl. Aileen noted that this might be a sensitive area, so she decided to skip the part of Alex's story in which he described how Tracy had got the boy to reveal the address of the house he visited. Alex said that Steven had also told the girl that the man who lived there had a trunk filled with treasure which he kept in an upstairs room, but the police seemed to feel that this unlikely detail must have been invented by Alex to justify what happened next.

'When you got home after your newspaper round that week,' Aileen resumed, 'Dave and Alex took you upstairs to the room where they'd hidden Jimmy's body and locked you in. Then they all went to the house in Grafton Avenue. The girl kept watch in the street while Dave and Alex went to the door and rang the bell in a special way you'd talked about.'

Steve suddenly twisted to one side in another convulsive shiver. Aileen waited, but he said nothing.

'When Mr Matthews opened the door, they pushed their way in and told him to show them where he had hidden his money. He gave them about thirty pounds, which he said was all he had. But Dave didn't believe him. He searched the house, looking for a trunk full of money which he thought was hidden there. When he couldn't find it he got very angry. First he threatened the old man with a poker, and then when Mr Matthews still wouldn't say where the money was, Dave started to hit him.'

'No!'

Steve spat the word at her.

'It wasn't him! It was the other one, the one with eyes that glow in the dark and burn you up! I seen him just before, just around the corner! He was on his way home after doing it. He opened him up like you're supposed to, tapping and tapping, only he was wrong, it wasn't like a golf ball inside, it was all messy.'

Aileen frowned. She had had just about enough of the boy's amateur mad scenes.

'There's no point in going on pretending, Steven,' she said sharply. 'I know you're trying to protect the others, but there's no need. Dave has already confessed. At first he denied knowing you and Alex, but the police showed your photograph to the security guards at the Tesco supermarket and one of them recognized it. He said you used to go there every week, and he remembered that one week two youths had an argument with you at the checkout. He was taken to the police station where he identified Dave and Alex. After that Dave admitted everything.'

'But it wasn't him!' the boy insisted. 'Why won't you listen? Why won't anyone listen? *I* didn't listen either. I thought he was crazy. I thought it was all a story he'd made up. But it was all true! He killed the old man and now he's after me too! I saw him leaving. He knows I know just like he knew what he done to him in the wood. That's why I got to stay here, see? He won't come near hospitals. He told me.'

Aileen held the wild eyes with her own, trying to decode this jumble of words.

'Mr Matthews told you this man would leave you alone as long as you were in hospital?'

The boy nodded. Aileen tried to hide her satisfaction as the last piece of the puzzle dropped into place.

'Now listen, Steven, there's something else which you must know. When the crime was discovered, the police tried to trace Mr Matthews's relatives. It turned out that he hadn't got any, but in the process they found out quite a lot about him. When he was young, a long long time ago, Ernest Matthews was a soldier. There was a big war and lots of people were killed. Mr Matthews was badly wounded. It wasn't his body that was hurt but his mind. He was suffering from what's called battle fatigue. Shell-shock, they used to call it. You see, when things get too bad, too horrible and frightening, then after a while human beings break down and get ill. One of the things that happens is that they imagine that people are threatening them, trying to kill them. They go on thinking that even after the danger is over, when they're perfectly safe and surrounded by people who care for them. That's what happened to Ernest Matthews. He must have been very ill indeed, because he was sent to a special hospital and stayed there for almost twenty years.'

'But I *seen* him!' the boy cried. 'I told you what he looked like, didn't I? And I told him too, and he said that was him, the man that was after him!'

'But we can't believe everything Mr Matthews told you, Steven. You didn't know that at the time, of course. He was older than you, so you naturally believed what he said. Perhaps he even believed it himself. Perhaps he really did still think that someone was threatening his life. Or perhaps that was just a story that was no longer real to him, which he told you so that you would keep on going to visit him. Perhaps he was afraid that you might get bored going to see an ordinary old man, so he tried to make himself more interesting. We'll never know the answer to that. What we *do* know is that what happened had nothing whatever to do with any story he may have told you. Mr Matthews was killed by a violent and unpredictable youth called Dave who had already murdered his friend Jimmy and had nothing to lose by killing again, particularly since he thought that the old man had a lot of money hidden in the house which he could use to get away. That's who killed Mr Matthews, Steven, not some character from a story. I think you know that. It's difficult for you to admit it, even to yourself. But one day, perhaps quite soon, you'll realize that there is no reason for you to feel guilty. Because that's the problem, isn't it? You feel guilty. If it hadn't been for you, Dave and Alex would never have heard about Mr Matthews and so he would still be alive. That's what you think, isn't it? It's almost as though you killed the old man yourself.'

This, she thought, is to proper psychiatric practice what an amputation with a handsaw and a tot of rum is to modern surgery. But there was no time, no money, and a queue of mutilated psyches bleeding to death at the hospital gate.

'But of course that's all nonsense! You never harmed the old man. On the contrary, you were his friend, you helped him. Even if you did tell the others where he lived, you couldn't possibly have known what they were going to do, could you? It had nothing whatever to do with you.'

The boy had resumed his unnatural stillness, locking himself away somewhere deep inside where he thought he could never be traced. Aileen shifted her grip on his arm, patting his wrist lightly.

'Let me tell you a little story, Steven. One day I was driving home from work when a cat suddenly ran out across the road in front of me. I tried to avoid it, but there was a car coming the other way. I heard a noise under the car and felt a bump. When I stopped and got out, the cat was dead.'

She moved a little closer to the boy, secure in her control of the situation, her mastery of the requisite skills.

'I felt awful, just terrible! I've always loved cats more than any other animal and yet I'd just killed one. It was such a horrible shock that it took me ages to realize that it wasn't my fault. There was absolutely nothing I could have done to prevent it. It took a long, long time to accept that, but in the end I managed to come to terms with it and stopped blaming myself uselessly.'

She tugged at the inert body beside her, trying without success to draw his eyes back to her.

'Now, of course, the shock you suffered was very much worse than mine, but one day the same thing will happen to you, too. It may take a long time, but one day you'll realize that it's all over. The past is dead, Steven. It's over and done with, finished. We can't reach it and it can't reach us. All we can do is to try and forget and think about today and tomorrow instead. Now I know that being here has helped you, and that's why I've arranged for you to go on coming every day, even though you'll be leaving this afternoon to go to a new home which Mrs Haynes has – '

'You're putting me out?'

The boy's face had gone to pieces again, all his composure fled at the notion of being expelled from his hard-won sanctuary.

'No, not at all,' Aileen speciously assured him. 'You'll be brought back here every morning and you'll spend the whole day doing all the things you've been doing up to now. The only thing that's going to change is that you won't actually sleep here any more.'

Steven stared at her bleakly. 'I can't stay?'

'No, Steven. You can't stay.'

It was better that he should be quite clear about that, she thought. It would only make matters worse if he were allowed to harbour false hopes.

'And you mustn't think of pretending to set fire to your new home, either,' she added, 'or they'll just hand you over to the police.'

After a long pause, a small bent smile appeared on the boy's lips, the first that Aileen had ever seen there. It startled her, because it was the absolute image of the way Raymond used to smile when he was about to say or do something mischievous.

'I'll have to be brave little Stevie, then,' he remarked. Encouraged and relieved at this response, Aileen smiled too.

'That's right,' she said warmly. 'Try to be brave. I know how it's hard, but – '

'Do you think I'll get in the papers?'

'The papers?'

She was lost.

'For being brave. They often used to have brave kids, the papers did. Brave means they're going to die. Like when they get the wrong disease or something, and there's no room at the hospital.'

Aileen gripped the boy's arm tightly.

'Steven, you must stop dramatizing like this! It's absurb to compare yourself with someone suffering from a fatal illness. You are not going to die, I promise you that. Certainly you're to be pitied, certainly you need care and attention. But no one wants to harm you, no one wishes you anything but good.'

The professional in Aileen recognized that the moment had come to terminate the interview. There was nothing more she could achieve for the moment. It was time for Steven to start the long hard work of facing the facts. Recovery from a serious delusion state is a rather like coming off heavy drink or drugs. Deprived of the flash romance and sinister glitter of your fantasies, life looks pretty dull and drab at first. It's terrible to believe that everyone is out to get you, but that way at least you're the centre of attention. It can be almost more terrible to have to accept that most people simply don't give a damn one way or the other. Meanwhile she had her own life to get on with. Friday afternoons were always particularly fraught: not only was it the moment when the things she had been putting off all week finally caught up with her, but there was also a large helping of bureaucratic roughage in the form of interdepartmental seminars, meetings of consultative review bodies and the like, which tested her boredom threshold to the limit. Nevertheless, regarded as occupational therapy the afternoon was a complete success, for Aileen thought no more about Steven Bradley until she was back in her office preparing to go home, and then it was only to congratulate herself on a job well done. Only that morning she had felt reality slipping away from her like the sand sucked out from under your feet by the waves on a beach. 'Here I go,' she'd thought. It had seemed so easy and restful to give in and stop trying to make sense of things. But she hadn't. That was a victory to celebrate, a success to reinforce. Perhaps she should treat herself to a concert or an evening at the theatre. When she got home, she'd check the paper and see what was on.

She was half-way out of the door when Mrs Haynes phoned.

'You haven't seen Steven, have you?'

The social worker sounded breathless.

'Seen him?' Aileen snapped. 'You were supposed to be collecting him at three o'clock.'

'I was! I did!'

'Well?'

'Well, he . . . he ran away.'

'He *what*?'

'I was driving him to the hostel, the traffic was quite bad – well, it always is these days, isn't it? Anyway, Gary, I mean Steven, he said he knew a short cut so I turned off, even though it seemed to me that it wasn't all that short – '

'Would you mind getting to the point, please?'

Aileen's tone of voice was a replica of one her mother used to intimidate people she considered socially vulnerable.

'Well, all of a sudden he said he needed to go to the loo. We were just passing a park and he said there was a public lavatory by the gate so I stopped. When he didn't come out again I went to the door and called. It was a bit awkward, it being a Gents and all, but in the end I went in but he wasn't there. I knew he hadn't come out of the door because I'd been watching, and then I saw that the window in one of the sit-downs was broken. He must have got out that way and run off through the park. I hoped he might have gone back there to the hospital, you see, that's why I phoned.'

Aileen squeezed the bridge of her nose between two fingers.

'Why would he come here? He knows we'd just hand him straight back to you.'

'But then where could he have gone?' the social worker wailed. She too was probably exhausted and drained at the end of a long week's work, Aileen reflected.

'I don't know. He showed some interest in a girl he used to know. He may have gone off looking for her. Anyway, don't worry too much, Mrs Haynes. It's not really your fault. He'd probably have run off sooner or later anyway. He's got a history of this kind of thing.'

She replaced the receiver, gathered together her belongings and walked slowly to the car. She knew only too well where Steven had gone. He had gone back to the street, back to the invisible people. The boy had tried to find his feet in the surface world, where people have fixed addresses and permanent names. But that world and its representatives, notably Aileen, had failed him. He had made his needs quite clear, and they had been rejected. And although that rejection was correct in the circumstances, Aileen's heart was tormented with reproachful questions. What did it matter to Steven whether he had an adequate claim to a hospital bed or not? Does a mother turn a child away because its need for security exceeds the norm, because it has exhausted its quota of love? But, of course, she wasn't his mother.

As Pamela Haynes had remarked, the traffic in the area was always bad. That afternoon, when Aileen longed more than ever to be home, it seemed by some perverse logic to be even worse than usual. Frustrated and bored, the occupants of the stalled cars gazed vacantly at each other, sizing up make, model, age and condition and hence inferring career, status, income level and probable destination. Aileen felt the eyes scanning her like so many remote-control video cameras: L registration Mini, ropy bodywork, sixty thousand or so on the clock, she's a bit second-hand and all, minor civil servant or administrative assistant, hit her plateau and stuck there, fifteen thou plus a few rubbishy perks, three kids and a semi in Greenford. She turned on the car radio. As she closed her eyes, the traffic jam melted away and they were cruising along the cliffs at

Rottingdean, sunlight flickering and glittering on the waves as though the ocean were signalling to them. 'What's it saying?' Ray shouted back. She hadn't needed to answer. They both knew by heart the exultant and irresistible message that the universe had confided to their generation. The whole of human history had been leading up to this moment, when technology and consciousness finally reached a sufficiently advanced level to make possible the earthly paradise. Ray laughed and took his hands off the bars, letting the motorbike steer itself around the curves of the road winding eastwards along the cliffs, towards Newhaven and the ferry.

'The Cream from 1969!' frothed the announcer. 'Wow, man, out of sight, too much, heavy, far out and all that stuff.'

Aileen swallowed away the lump of emotion in her throat. A chorus of horns sounded out behind her, and she looked up to find that the vehicle in front had moved forward a few yards. Before she could put the Mini in gear, a brand-new Ford Sierra cut into the space. The driver waved angrily at her as he passed, mouthing inaudible oaths, his eyes full of hatred. High-stress middle management, twenty-five thousand plus a company ulcer, new home on a Wates estate in Uxbridge, thought Aileen automatically.

About half-way along Wood Lane there was a way through the back streets avoiding Shepherds Bush Green. The snag was getting out again the other end, which was why Aileen didn't often use it, but today the traffic was so bad that she couldn't see what she had to lose. As she drew near the junction, however, she saw that the traffic this end was not moving at all. After sitting there for ten minutes without progressing an inch, she backed the Mini into a parking space and got out. There was a nice Young's pub round the corner. She would go and relax over a drink and a cigarette until the rush-hour had passed.

About fifty yards along the main road, a knot of people blocked her path. A policeman was questioning some of them while another stood in the road directing the traffic. Aileen became aware of a siren in the distance and realized that it had been going on for some time without her noticing it. It was presumably an ambulance, stuck in the traffic jam caused by the accident to which it had been called. A white delivery van was stopped at an angle in the middle of the road, almost on the white line. Behind it stood a bus, stalled at the moment of pulling away from its stop. One of the men being questioned gestured towards the van.

'He didn't give me a bleeding chance, did he?'

'How fast were you going?' the policeman asked, pencil and notebook at the ready.

'I don't know! Twenty, twenty-five? It's a van, not a bleeding Ferrari, you know. Just as I was passing the bus, out he comes like a dog out of the trap.'

'That's right,' the bus driver confirmed. He pointed out a man standing nearby. 'Him over there, he said something made him run off.'

Everyone turned to look at the man. Amid all the faces marked by anxiety or sorrow, the grin on his lips struck a jarring note. The policeman beckoned him over.

'What did you say to him?'

The man laughed almost contemptuously.

'Nothing!'

'You bloody well did!' the bus driver exclaimed. 'I saw you!'

The man looked as though he was only able to restrain his hilarity because not even the most hysterical howls of laughter would be adequate to express the total absurdity of the situation. The whole thing was simply *too* stupid for words!

'What did you say to him?' the policeman repeated coldly.

The man shrugged three or four times in quick succession.

'I asked if he knew what time it was.'

'That's right,' a woman with a dog put in. 'I heard him.'

The policeman looked rather exasperated by the woman's unsolicited testimony.

'What's so funny?' he snapped at the man, whose grin vanished with insulting abruptness.

'Where do you live?' the policeman demanded.

'Paxton Grove. Number twenty-nine.'

Up to this point, Aileen had been hovering on the fringes of the crowd, trying to work her way through. Now she stopped and gave the man a closer look. 29 Paxton Grove was a custodial hostel used to accommodate long-term psychiatric patients whose condition was more or less stable but unlikely to improve. This man was pretty obviously a chronic schizophrenic whose symptoms were being controlled by drugs sufficiently for him to be released into the community.

'Excuse me, I'm a doctor,' she told the policeman, exaggerating her qualifications to get his attention. 'I think I may be able to help.'

He glanced at her briefly and shook his head, pointing towards a blanket-covered bundle lying in the road in front of the white van.

'Too late for that.'

Aileen was about to explain that she wasn't that kind of doctor but simply wanted to explain why the man being questioned was acting so oddly, but something about the size of the covered form drew her towards it. Her assumed status as a doctor cleared a passage for her through the crowd, and the police made no move to interfere as she bent to pull back the corner of the blanket. The boy's head had been broken open and the face smeared like a wet painting, but there was no doubt as to his identity. Steven Bradley's brief flight was over.

THIRTEEN

She turned away, towards the traffic squeezing slowly past the scene of the accident. A bus was inching its way through the gap between the delivery van in the middle of the road and the line of parked cars opposite. As it passed her, Aileen stepped on to the open platform, went inside and sat down on one of the bench seats. Once clear of the obstacle, the bus accelerated away. The other passengers – a mother and her two children, an old man with a small dog, two pale working-class girls and an Asian youth in a two-tone tracksuit – all turned to face the front again. Overhead, boots pounded on the upper deck. 'We're *com*-in'! We're *com*-in'!' voices chanted rhythmically.

'Fares, please.'

'Stamford Brook,' Aileen replied automatically.

'Don't go there.' The conductor was an elderly black, his voice and gestures robotic with exhaustion. 'Change in Acton. Fifty pence.'

Aileen handed him the coins.

'I couldn't do anything about it,' she said. 'He ran straight out in front of me.'

The drumming overhead intensified.

'*SCOT*-land! *SCOT*-land!'

The conductor handed her the ticket.

'It wasn't my fault,' Aileen explained. 'That's why I've stopped blaming myself, you see.'

One of the working girls turned to stare at her. Then she whispered something to her friend and they both tittered. There was a clatter of boots on the stairs and two youths in T-shirts and skin-tight jeans appeared, waving open cans of lager. One of them had a Scottish flag draped around his shoulders. He waved his fist at the conductor.

'Hey, you black jobbie, did you no' hear the bell?'

Aileen took hold of his arm.

'You're going to die,' she told him. 'I promise you that.'

A can of McEwan's wrapped in knuckles ornamented with swastikas and death's heads swayed back and forth in the air a few inches from Aileen's face.

'You's barmy, woman,' he said, backing away.

The gob of white foam had pushed up through the keyhole-shaped opening in the can. It made Aileen think of the cuckoo-spittle that used to appear suddenly in spring. The long grasses by the stream were all spattered with the stuff. She would lie there for hours, hidden from view, sharing a sinful cigarette with her friend Liz. The clouds scudded along overhead, and in the windswept space between a lark was ecstatically soloing. Her mother used to tell a story about children from London who were evacuated to the Cotswolds during the war. 'One day, one of the boys came home in great excitement. "There's a little sparrer stuck up there!" he said. "He can't get up and he can't get down, and he ain't half making a fuss about it!" The little Cockney had never seen a skylark before in his life, you see!'

When Aileen looked again, the youths had gone. At the next stop, the two girls got up and walked towards the platform with short rapid strides, hobbled at the knee by their tight acrylic skirts. As they passed Aileen they broke into suppressed giggles that turned into howls of laughter as soon as they were off the bus. From time to time the bus stopped and people got on or off. Eventually Aileen stood up.

'Not this one,' warned the conductor.

'It's all right,' she replied. 'I know my way.'

Once off the bus, however, the streets seemed unfamiliar. Still, if she kept walking she would get home sooner or later. Occasionally a dog barked in one of the houses as she passed, or she overheard music or the abrupt roar of recorded laughter, or saw lights left on in an empty room. Of course, all these phenomena could have been simulated by devices such as the one that Douglas had installed.

As it began to get dark, she found herself in a long avenue built on a slight curve. The houses had windows consisting of eight panes set in a curved bay, and whenever a car approached, its headlights caught the panes one after the other, making the windows flash like warning beacons. But a few hundred yards further on, everything became familiar again, and the only puzzle was how it could have previously looked so strange. Aileen supposed it was due to her having taken an unfamiliar route. Even a place you know well can look odd if approached from an unfamiliar direction. She didn't think about it much, preoccupied with her enjoyment at having got home safely. In spite of all that had happened, she was looking forward immensely to getting inside and shutting the door behind her, to eating and drinking and watching TV. Life goes on, she told herself. That's all it does. It goes on, until it stops.

As she approached the front door, searching through her handbag for her keys, the phone started ringing inside. It would probably be Douglas, ringing to say that he had arrived safely. How nice of him! She felt very warm about Douglas sometimes, particularly when he wasn't there. Her hand blindly rooted about in the bag, turning up her purse and diary, various items of make-up, two letters and a packet of tissues, but no keys. The ringing broke off with a truncated blip. She imagined Douglas setting down the receiver and turning away, disappointed or angry or even worried. As for the keys, she'd left them in the door of the Mini, of course.

Driving with Raymond in the mountains north of Los Angeles, Aileen had noticed that almost every bend in the road was marked by a black sign with one or more death's heads painted on it. Raymond had explained that each skull marked the scene of a fatal accident. But when her taxi reached the spot where Steven Bradley had died a few hours earlier, there was no sign that anything of any interest or importance had ever taken place there. Aileen paid the driver and walked around the corner to the place where she had left the Mini. It wasn't there. With it had gone the keys to her house, whose address was marked on several of the letters and other documents she had left on the back seat. That meant it wouldn't be safe to go home, but before the implications of this had sunk in she saw Steven. He came at her like a wolf, swooping across the street straight in front of a car that never swerved an inch to avoid him, just as though he wasn't there. Aileen screamed at him again and again, trying to scare him off, until people appeared at the windows of the nearby houses to see what was the matter.

She was in luck: the taxi that had brought her to the corner was still there, parked at the kerb, the driver counting his takings. At first he said he was off duty, but when Aileen told him where she wanted to go he smirked and nodded her into the back. The taxi dropped her at the side of the main block, by the sign 'WARNING HAZCHEM'. The night staff were very sympathetic about the loss of her car and keys. They provided tea and biscuits and said of course she could spend the night. In the morning, Aileen knew, everything would be all right again. But first there was the night to get through. Before going to bed she paid a visit to the dispensary and took some Valium. Mindful of what had happened last time, she restricted herself to the manufacturer's suggested dose, even though her room was in the basement and the window had bars on it.

In other respects, the experience was not dissimilar. She awoke in broad daylight, in a hospital. No one mentioned miracles this time, but of course miracles only happen once. Most striking of all, she'd had the flying dream again, and this time it lingered tantalizingly on the fringes of her consciousness. The merest nudge, she felt, would be enough to bring it back into focus. But her waking consciousness was too gross and clumsy an instrument, and a few moments later it was impossible to believe that the experience hadn't all been an illusion. She washed and dressed, drank several cups of tea, thanked the staff and set out to walk to the tube. It was a warm and sunny day, and her mood had changed too. In fact a miracle of sorts *had* occurred, after all, for she felt sane again. She knew that she had been in shock the evening before, and had acted pretty oddly. But all that was over now.

Her mood was briefly marred by the discovery, when she reached the tube station, that she had left her handbag behind at the hospital. Evidently some of the Valium must still be spicing her chemical soup, making her dopey and inattentive. For a moment she thought of going back to get it, but it was a long way through an unattractive part of West Kilburn. Besides, there was nothing of any value in the bag. Her money and credit cards were in her purse, which she had put in her coat pocket after paying the taxi driver the night before. The real problem was the loss of her keys. She would have to inform the police, then call a locksmith. It would take the whole day, just when she felt she needed a rest, peace and quiet.

It wasn't until she reached Paddington that she understood what she was going to do. Coming up from the underground tunnels to change to the District line, she caught sight of a sign reading 'Main Line Station'. Without a second thought, she followed the arrow, made her way to the booking office and bought a weekend return to Cheltenham. It was the perfect solution! She tried to phone her parents before boarding the train, but the phones were all in use or out of order. It didn't matter, anyway. They would be only too pleased to see her, even though she turned up unannounced with nothing but the clothes she stood up in. They would understand, bless them. They always did. And from there she would phone the police, report the theft of her car keys and ask them to keep an eye on the house. It would be bliss to get out of London for a couple of days, to go home. It was just what she needed.

The train was scruffy, blisteringly hot and packed. Aileen put her coat on the overhead rack and squeezed into a corner seat, where she lay back and closed her eyes. When she awoke, they were already in the country. Bright sunlight fell on flat farmland with a roll of low hills in the distance. The carriage had emptied somewhat, although it was still quite crowded. On the seat opposite, a man with a smugly glum expression was leafing through a newspaper with the headline 'LEAVE IT AHT, RON!' Next to him, in the window seat, a relentlessly articulate middle-class father was talking the toddler on his knee through the scene outside, naming all the buildings and animals, explaining their functions and purpose, instructing his creation in the various amenities of a world that had been brought into being for his benefit.

Aileen slept in short snatches, during which the scene outside gradually changed from the bleak expanses of chalk and clay to the secretive limestone landscape she knew so well: valleys that seemed too big for the limpid streams lined with elms and willows, meadows full of unbothered sheep, villages that seemed to have been exposed by a process of erosion. Inside the train they were still in London, while out there, just the other side of the glass streaked with urban filth, was a whole countryside so intimately linked to Aileen's childhood that for her it would never quite grow up.

When she next opened her eyes, the train had come to a stop in a small station. Sunlight fell hot and heavy on the seat where she was sitting, bringing out sweat under the light cotton dress which had seemed too scanty just the day before. Further down the carriage a portable stereo was dispensing a slouching reggae beat over which a rap artist was doing vocal karate. The seat opposite was now occupied by a harassed-looking mother and child. The mother was staring out of the window with an obstinate expression, pointedly ignoring the child, a girl of about six with a face like a blancmange, who was crying loudly.

'Don't make such a fuss!' her mother snapped.

She can't get up and she can't get down, thought Aileen, that's the problem. But she was careful not to say anything. The music gouged and stabbed, the child cried, the train did not move. There seemed no reason why it should ever move again. Sunlight streamed in through the grimy window, making the carriage unbearably hot and airless. The bawling child and the ghetto-blaster competed gamely for attention. No one else seemed bothered by any of this, but Aileen felt that if she stayed there a minute longer she would go mad. She opened the door and stepped out on to the platform, determined to find out what was going on and how much longer they were going to have to wait there. Outside the train, the air was deliciously cool and fresh, delicately scented. The sunlight was light and gentle, modulated by a slight breeze, no longer a penance.

'Hey!' A man in uniform waved at her from the next carriage. 'Get back in!'

'I beg your pardon?' Aileen replied icily.

'You can't get off here! The train doesn't stop here.'

The only advantage of living with a complete bastard, Aileen had realized, was that it gave you a head start in dealing with all the other bastards you came across in the course of your everyday life. The guard's words made her remember one evening when she had made the mistake of greeting Douglas's early return with, 'Oh, I thought you were still at work.' She hadn't forgotten his crushing rejoinder.

'There are doubtless various ingenious ways of demonstrating that you're mistaken,' she told the guard airily. 'But under the circumstances it may be sufficient to point out that the train *has* stopped and that I *have* got off.'

The man didn't respond, and at that moment the train started to move again. In the same instant Aileen realized what he had meant. This was not a normal stop but a disused station where the train had come to a halt waiting for a signal to change. The platform at her feet was still more or less intact, with the odd plant pushing up between the slabs, but the nameboards had been removed and the station building looked as though it had been hit by a shell.

The train disappeared round a bend and the signal changed soundlessly back to red. Aileen laughed to herself. It served her right! She'd been hoist with her own petard, or rather with Douglas's, which she'd ill-advisedly borrowed. There was nothing for it but to walk to the nearest village and phone her parents. She couldn't be far from home now and fortunately her father was always glad of an excuse to take the car out. 'But what on earth happened?' he would ask. 'Well,' she'd reply, 'it's a long story!' She climbed through the slack barbed-wire fence which separated the platform from the station yard, and began to walk up the drive, the gravel crunching under her feet. It was hard to feel annoyed by what had happened when it had brought her this quiet, these scents and sounds, the wonderful sunlight and this breeze that ruffled the little golden hairs on her arms.

The track joined a narrow lane that crossed the stream and the railway and started to climb the other side of the valley. The verges were dense with overgrown vegetation, an impenetrable clutter of spindly tendrils matted together, bending under their own weight. Aileen had once feared the approach of winter, but now she found it a relief to think that all this superfluous growth would soon be swept away. It seemed almost threatening in its mindless proliferation. After a while the lane joined a wider road, boasting a white line in the middle. A signpost indicated one village five and three-quarter miles to the left and another half a mile to the right. On the other side of the road stood an imposing pair of stone gateposts, one of which bore a sign lettered in gold on a blue ground.

Netherbourne Hall
Golden Age Sheltered Accommodation

Beneath this, a separate notice read 'No Through Road'. Through the gates, Aileen could see an Elizabethan manor house with gables, mock crenellation, traceried windows and clusters of tall chimney-stacks, all in the local honey-coloured stone. It looked vaguely familiar. No doubt she had come here at some time with her parents, on a Sunday afternoon drive. Perhaps she could phone from there, she thought. If it was an old people's home it couldn't be strictly private. There would always be relatives coming to visit. The drive curved sinuously away to the right through fenced-off parkland where sheep were grazing. Clouds occasionally drifted over the sun, muting the colours and casting a cool dull spell over the scene. As Aileen got closer to the house, she began to feel uneasy about going in. They must be fed up with people sneaking around the place with some feeble excuse or other, taking pictures. But by now she had come so far that it would be quicker to detour across the lawn and try and find a way out to the village, which according to the signpost lay only half a mile away in that direction.

Even the Macklins' next-door neighbour, the exacting Mr Griffiths, might have approved of the lawn, a magnificent expanse of grass trimmed in perfectly straight strips, except where circular flowerbeds had been planted around the stumps of two trees whose roots presumably went too deep for them to be removed without damage. Aileen strolled across it, glancing nervously at the grey stone façade of the house. She was afraid that at any moment one of the many windows would open with a bang and someone lean out and demand to know who she was and where she was going. Nothing of the sort happened, however. In a few moments she had reached the path, which led past the end of the opposite wing into a glade of enormous rhododendron plants. Beyond stood a small church, and Aileen decided to go in and have a look. Her mother knew every church for miles around, and if this one turned out to have a thirteenth-century font or a perfectly preserved hammerbeam roof Aileen would never hear the end of it. She was already starting to worry about what to say to her parents.

She walked through the lych-gate and up the path that curved past tumbling tombstones covered in elegant but largely illegible lettering. The porch was protected by a screen-door to keep out birds. This was open, but she wondered whether the church itself would be. So many were kept locked these days, a thing unheard of when she and her parents had done their tours. 'The house of God is always open,' she remembered her mother saying sententiously, and then making a disapproving noise when her husband added, 'Unlike the public houses, alas.' Aileen grasped the ring of braided iron set in the massive door and turned. There was a loud clack and the door swung back. The place smelt as ripely musty as a cellar. A pile of hymnals stood on a low table near the door, below a notice-board displaying a photograph of a drought victim in Africa and a faded typewritten note explaining that a service was held there on the fourth Sunday of every alternate month.

She walked slowly around. The church had evidently been subject to some pretty brutal restoration, and its most striking feature was a set of memorials to the local gentry spanning some three hundred years. The earliest was a statue of an Elizabethan gentleman leaning on his elbow with an expression of fastidious boredom, as if death were the last in a long series of social duties which he had undertaken without enthusiasm or complaint. After that the style turned chilly and classical for a century or so, all marble urns and garlands, before Victorian earnestness took over. The last plaque, near the door, was a brass plate with incised red and black lettering. It commemorated two brothers: Rupert Jeffries, 1898 – 1916, *Dulce et decorum est pro patria mori*, and Maurice Jeffries, 1898 – , *Et in Arcadia ego*. The missing date seemed rather bizarre, as though suggesting that the person concerned might not really be dead. The little leaflet on the history of the church, which Aileen found on the table next to the hymnals and for which she was urged to make a contribution of 'at least 6d', proved unhelpful. It mentioned only that the Hall had been uninhabited for some time following the deaths of both heirs to the estate during the Great War and was now, 'like so many of our great country houses, virtually derelict'. It was only when she made to put her contribution in the collecting box that Aileen realized that her purse was in the pocket of her coat, which she had left on the rack in the train.

Outside, the sky had clouded over quite considerably. It had grown almost uncomfortably close. The loss of her purse was a blow, for although it only contained about ten pounds, it was all she had with her. The attractions of this improvised day in the country were rapidly beginning to fade. She would have to find a phone box and make a reversed charge call, but first she had to find the way into the village. Regaining the path she had been on before, she came to another imposing set of gates leading out of the estate. Unlike the ones by which she had entered, however, these were locked and chained and clearly no longer in use. This was doubly frustrating, because she could see the rooftops of the village through the foliage beyond the gates, not more than a few hundred yards away. There was no way out, however. The alternatives were to return the way she had come, to take a narrow path to the right marked 'Staff Only', or to turn left up a track which skirted the wall of the estate. This seemed to offer the best possibility of finding a short cut to the village, and Aileen started along it.

The track was at first covered in gravel, but this soon gave way to a rough surface of dried mud, deeply rutted, with a strip of grass and wild flowers in the middle. The parkland surrounding the manor house gradually turned to rough meadow as the track had started to climb the open hillside. This proved surprisingly steep, and despite her impatience to get to a phone, Aileen found herself pausing frequently for breath, once even taking the opportunity to pick some overripe blackberries from the bushes in the ditching beside the track. The berries burst as she pulled them off, staining her fingers. Afterwards she wished she had left them alone, for she had nothing to wipe her hands on. It was already going to be difficult enough to come up with a story to tell her parents without making herself sound totally scatty. The last thing she needed was to turn up with her hands and dress apparently stained with blood. There was no sign of any path or road leading off to the village. The track ran straight ahead to the top of the hill. Aileen kept looking about her as she walked, hoping to find a bit of waste paper she could clean her hands on, but the only things she saw were useless to her: a work glove of some shiny red rubberized material lying palm up on the ground, and a large piece of torn plastic marked Gro-More, which had become trapped in the barbed-wire fencing and was flapping loudly in the wind. Finally she came to a dew-pond beside the track, a deep crater lined with black plastic sheeting. As she bent to wash the blackberry juice off her hands, she caught sight of her reflection in the water. She looked frail and fragile. The sleeveless white dress clung to her body like a shift. She put her hands into the water, blurring the image.

The land to either side grew barer and more exposed as she neared the crest of the hill. The traditional drystone walls had been swept away to create large efficient spaces for the cereal crop whose severed stalks covered the ground. Clouds of smoke started drifting across the track, light and tenuous at first, then suddenly thick, billowing and impenetrable. It looked as though some tremendous disaster had taken place. There were flames blended in with the smoke, orange turning to brown or brilliant red. The air was filled with their crackling. When the smoke thinned for a moment, Aileen saw figures running about with pitchforks, carrying smouldering straw to spread the blaze to the unburnt stubble. But they were too far away for her to ask for directions, and the next moment the wind changed direction, plunging her back into the smoke, which grew so thick that she could only see intermittently. When the smoke finally cleared, Aileen paused to take stock of her situation. The track she was on looked like one of the old drove-roads which continued for miles across the hills without passing any human habitation. The clouds were getting thicker and darker every moment: it was pretty obviously going to pour with rain in the not-too-distant future. About fifty yards further on there was a farmhouse standing beside the track, and rather than walking all the way back again, Aileen decided to go and ask for directions. They might know of a footpath down to the village, or even have a phone she could use. As the building grew nearer, Aileen was surprised to see how impressive it was for an outlying tenant farm. It had three storeys, with large gables, and was built of the local stone, richly mottled with lichen. Even more surprising, it appeared to be derelict. A new corrugated iron barn had been erected nearby and was being used to store various pieces of farm machinery, but the house itself seemed to be abandoned. The garden was a wilderness, several of the windows were smashed and the front door stood open.

The first sign she had of what was happening was when the dust at her feet suddenly started to flick up into the air and the first drops struck her arms. A moment later the rain was pelting down and her dress had turned a shade darker. She ran into the garden of the house and took shelter under an enormous yew tree growing there. The rain hung across the landscape as thick as a curtain, blown in folds by the wind. Already the track had turned into a stream flowing back towards the valley. With the gusting wind, the yew provided scant shelter. Aileen now saw that a path of sorts had been cleared through the nettles and long grass to the front door of the farmhouse. As the storm showed no sign of slackening for the moment, she decided to make a dash for it.

Once across the threshold, everything was dry and hushed and still. The place seemed at first to be in reasonably good order, which only increased the mystery of why it was uninhabited, given the property values in the area these days. But as soon as she started looking around, it became clear that this was an illusion. There had been no vandalism or wanton destruction: the house had just started to collapse under its own weight. The hallway and stairs were still intact, but the other rooms were a shambles, the flagstones of the floor covered in fallen joists and chunks of lath and plaster. Aileen stood looking about at the vast space above her head, cleared of all partitions, listening to the wind roaring in the cavernous fireplace and the rattle of rain against the leaded window panes. She felt very tired suddenly, deeply weary. She longed to be home. Then, quite distinctly, high overhead, she heard a cry.

Slowly and calmly, as though she had been expecting this, Aileen turned and made her way back to the hall, stepping carefully over the lengths of wood and lumps of plaster on the floor. Outside in the garden, the yew was tossing to and fro like a head in pain, but within the house all was still. When she gripped the banister her hand came away covered in dirt, and the stairs creaked loudly as she started to climb them. They advanced towards a blind wall, then reversed direction and continued up to a landing lit by one of the broken windows. It was only when she looked to her left, through a doorway that opened on to nothing, that Aileen felt any fear. But even then it was only for a moment, and the cry she had heard was constantly repeated, plaintive and pleading, impossible to ignore. The next set of stairs was narrower and steeper, one long, continuous flight spanning the entire width of the house. The steps were tall and heavily worn and the bare plaster wall was discoloured by rubbing shoulders, as though generations had passed that way. Gradually Aileen's body blocked out the light from the window below until she could see nothing. She groped forward into the darkness, where her outstretched hands encountered a rough wooden surface. Beyond it, the cry sounded again and again, louder and more urgent than before. Aileen pushed and struck the door in vain, almost panicking as she failed to find any handle. Then her frantic fingers stumbled on a latch set high up. As soon as she pressed the release, the door sprang open like a trap and something came straight at her face, speedy and mobile, inhumanly crying. She threw herself to one side, holding up her hands to protect her face. At the last moment the bird veered round in a tight curve and flew straight at one of the windows. It struck the glass hard and fell to the floor, where it fluttered about dazedly, uttering its mournful cry.

The attic ran the whole length and width of the house, an expanse of bare planks lit by the three windows, one in each of the gables. Overhead, rafters supported the overlapping stone tiles of the roof. It was here, no doubt, that the bird had got in, slipping through a chink between two tiles. Unable to find its way out again, it was staring at Aileen with an expression which seemed full of pride and hurt, of baffled resentment. All she had to do was open one of the windows. She had covered about half the distance, moving slowly so as not to alarm the bird any further, when she heard something snap and felt a jolt underfoot. The bird promptly took to the air, perching on a tie-beam as the centre of the floor sagged several inches. When she tried to turn back, Aileen fell on her side, deceived by the slope of the boards. Under this impact the floor opened up completely, but Aileen was aware of this only for an instant. Then night fell, warm and black and luminous. The lawn stretched smoothly away, flowing out and around the two great beeches. The grass was heavy with dew, which gleamed flawlessly in the moonlight as she glided across it, her feet not touching the ground, the air softly lifting and enfolding her. The vision can have lasted only the few seconds that it took her falling body to reach the stone slabs below, but it was of such power and beauty that it seemed a more than adequate recompense for everything that had ever happened to her, and for whatever was about to happen.